CONTENTS

Pedigree Books Ltd, Beech Hill House, Walnut Gardens, Exeter, Devon EX4 4DH
www.pedigreebooks.com I books@pedigreegroup.co.uk I Published 2010.

£7.99

ASH & PIKACHU

SOME DAY I'M GONNA WIN THE SINNOH LEAGUE!

ASH Ketchum is the kind of pal we all dream of having around. The Trainer is plucky, kind and loyal to a fault! If he heard that a friend was in trouble, Ash would cross burning bridges to come to their rescue, dismissing the risks with a wave of his hand. In the past he's been called foolhardy and hot-headed, but wouldn't you want someone like Ash covering your back if you were to explore the mountainous Sinnoh region?

Ever since he can remember, Ash has wanted to become a Pokémon master. He's spent years perfecting his craft and learning about Pokémon behaviour, an education that he continues to this day. Even the shortest amount of downtime is seen as an opportunity to train and brush up on moves, maximising his chances of success in Gym Battle. Ash is very proud of the Gym Badges that he has won so far. Now that he's explored several regions, he's more determined than ever before to become the best of the best!

Ash likes to travel with a close team of friends that he can trust through thick and thin. When he set out as a bumbling Pallet Town novice, he was late arriving at Professor Oak's laboratory on his very first morning. Instead of selecting the Squirtle that he hoped for, Ash was introduced to Pikachu, the Electric-Type. This unusual starter Pokémon has become his best pal in the whole world. Ash also roams Sinnoh with Brock and Dawn, two friends and confidants that he can't do without.

PIKACHU

PIKACHU is an unlikely choice for a young Trainer, but over the years he has more than earnt his perch on Ash's shoulder. The Pokémon is very similar to his friend in many ways – a feisty, noble and fun-loving creature that people like to have around. At first there were fireworks between the duo, but after lots of scrapes and even more adventures the pair have built up a trust that's second to none.

Poor Pikachu is often vulnerable to attack, as he is such a rare and gifted Pokémon. Team Rocket constantly mount bids to snatch the Electric-Type from Ash, but Pikachu is more than able to defend himself. The smart little cookie uses his wit, guts and sparks to outwit even the most formidable opponents – living proof that bulk isn't always an indicator of strength and determination.

SECRET ASH FACT

ASH STARTED HIS POKÉMON JOURNEY WHEN HE WAS TEN-YEARS-OLD.

SECRET PIKACHU FACT

PIKACHU IS THE ONLY ONE OF ASH'S POKEMON NOT TO TRAVEL IN A POKÉ BALL

POKÉMON PALS

BROCK

LET'S GET COOKING!

Brock is Ash's oldest travelling companion, following the Trainer through the Kanto, Johto, Hoenn and Sinnoh regions. A former leader of the Pewter City Gym, Brock's life experiences have enabled him to build up an awesome knowledge of Pokémon species. A walking Pokédex with a passion for fine food, Brock dreams of one day becoming a recognised Pokémon Breeder. Breeders specialise in rearing and taming Pokémon young.

During the course of his journey with Dawn and Ash, Brock has built up his own trusty team of Pokémon. His faithful Croagunk always steps in if the Breeder gets too gooey-eyed with the ladies, while his Sudowoodo and Happiny can be counted on to defend their master from hostile attacks.

When he's not advising his pals on Pokémon behaviour, Brock loves to get busy in the kitchen. His camp cooking is delicious, as is his scrumptious secret poffin recipe. It's a hobby that grub-loving Ash is more than happy to endorse!

SECRET BROCK FACT

HE'S ALWAYS GOT VITAL INFORMATION IN HIS COLLECTION OF BOOKS AND MAPS

DAWN

NO NEED TO WORRY!

Ash and Brock first met Dawn in Twinleaf Town, just days after arriving in Sinnoh. This is her very first expedition away from home, but Dawn has loved every minute of her time on the road. The youngster has learnt heaps about Pokémon already, as well as collecting a few new friends of her own!

Her goal is to become a Co-ordinator, entering Contests where her Pokémon are judged on the beauty of their moves rather than the power of attack. Having said that, if there's trouble brewing Dawn will never back away from a fight. Her gutsy Piplup is always ready to leap to her defence too, even if the opponent is double its size.

Dawn's mother Johanna was a famed Pokémon Co-ordinator, so the apprentice is on a quest to make her family proud of her achievements too! Sometimes this can make Dawn rather over-excitable, but her smiling face never fails to spur Ash on when times are tough. Both he and Brock agree that she's the perfect third member of their Pokémon team!

SECRET DAWN FACT
DAWN'S LATEST NEW POKÉMON IS A MASSIVE AND UNRULY MAMOSWINE!

TEAM ROCKET

BRINGING CHAOS AT A BREAKNECK PACE!

During their spell in Sinnoh, Team Rocket have managed to make themselves universally unpopular. The threesome have rampaged the countryside, stealing Pokémon and sabotaging countless Contests and Gym Battles. Behind the rumpus are three deeply flawed characters, each one out to get what they can from Ash and his friends.

JESSIE

The purple-haired princess is the self-claimed leader of Team Rocket. Argumentative, vain and pushy, she will stop at nothing to get what she wants. Jessie is a master of disguise, often changing personas so that she can snatch Gym Badges or lure valuable Pokémon into her nasty clutches. Unfortunately for Jessie, she is totally talentless as a Co-ordinator and Trainer, a fact that she will never accept.

Jessie has got a shockingly short temper and a sharp tongue. Anyone who disappoints her does so at their personal peril!

JAMES

Weak-willed James is Team Rocket's resident snake-in-the-grass. Originally from a wealthy family, James quit his riches for a life of adventure and intrigue on the wrong side of the tracks. The floppy-fringed meanie is sly and calculating, always ready to snatch innocent Pokémon and sell them for a buck or two. At times, James can seem sentimental. He loves his Pokémon dearly and can never resist a good sob story. When it comes to stealing however, he's only got eyes for himself.

MEOWTH

Team Rocket's wise-cracking Meowth stands apart from most Pokémon. The talented baddie walks on two legs, communicating by human speech. Instead of putting these talents to good use however, the kitty uses its brains to launch elaborate Pokémon-snatching plots.

Meowth always talks a great talk, using his powers of persuasion to launch the most outrageous bids to gain money and influence. Unfortunately nearly all his schemes are doomed to failure from the outset. Meowth has lost count of the times that he and his partners-in-crime have been sent blasting off into oblivion. No matter what the situation, Team Rocket will manage to get things spectacularly wrong each and every time!

SECRET TEAM ROCKET FACT
THE TRIO'S UNDERGROUND BOSS IS A MYSTERIOUS CRIME LORD CALLED GIOVANNI.

POKÉ PRACTICE

Ash has come a long way from the impatient young apprentice who first set his sights on the goal of Pokémon master! It's taken many battles and countless training sessions for the Trainer to build up his knowledge, yet there's still so much more to learn.

Do you aspire to Pokémon greatness too? Warm yourself up with this easy multiple choice quiz, then flip forward to take the Grand Trainer Challenge on page 36.

Let's start with the basics...

3. WHAT DOES A POKÉMON BREEDER SPECIALISE IN?

A. MAKING SURE POKÉMON DON'T BREAK THE LAW ◯

B. WINNING POKÉMON DRESS-UP CONTESTS ◯

C. REARING YOUNG POKÉMON ◯

2. WHEN MAY TRAINERS RECEIVE THEIR FIRST STARTER POKÉMON?

A. ANY AGE ◯

B. 18 YEARS-OLD ◯

C. 10 YEARS-OLD ◯

1. WHERE DO SICK POKÉMON GET TREATED?

A. POKÉMON CENTRES ◯

B. FIRST AID ROOMS IN LOCAL SHOPPING MALLS ◯

C. REGULAR HOSPITALS ◯

4. WHO HANDLES POLICING IN THE POKÉMON WORLD?

A. OFFICER JOY ◯

B. OFFICER JENNY ◯

C. OFFICER MISTY ◯

5. WHAT DO POKÉMON TRAVEL IN?

A. THEIR OWNERS' RUCKSACKS ◯

B. POKÉ BALLS ◯

C. THEIR OWN LITTLE VEHICLES ◯

6. HOW MANY TIMES DO POKÉMON EVOLVE?

A. AT LEAST THREE TIMES ◯

B. ONLY ONCE ◯

C. IT VARIES WITH EVERY SPECIES ◯

9. WHAT TREAT DO POKÉMON LIKE TO EAT?

A. POFFINS ◯

B. MUFFINS ◯

C. DOUGHNUTS ◯

8. HOW DO POKÉMON TRAINERS WIN GYM BADGES?

A. BY WINNING A BATTLE AGAINST A GYM LEADER ◯

B. BY DEMONSTRATING THREE STRONG BATTLE MOVES ◯

C. BY SPENDING AT LEAST A MONTH IN A REGION ◯

7. WHAT DO TRAINERS USE TO FIND OUT ABOUT THE SPECIES THEY ENCOUNTER?

A. AN ENCYCLOPAEDIA ◯

B. A SPECIAL POKÉMON MAP ◯

C. A POKÉDEX ◯

10. HOW MANY KNOWN SPECIES OF POKÉMON ARE THERE?

A. CLOSE TO 1,000 ◯

B. CLOSE TO 100 ◯

C. CLOSE TO 500 ◯

How did you measure up? Write your score out of 10:

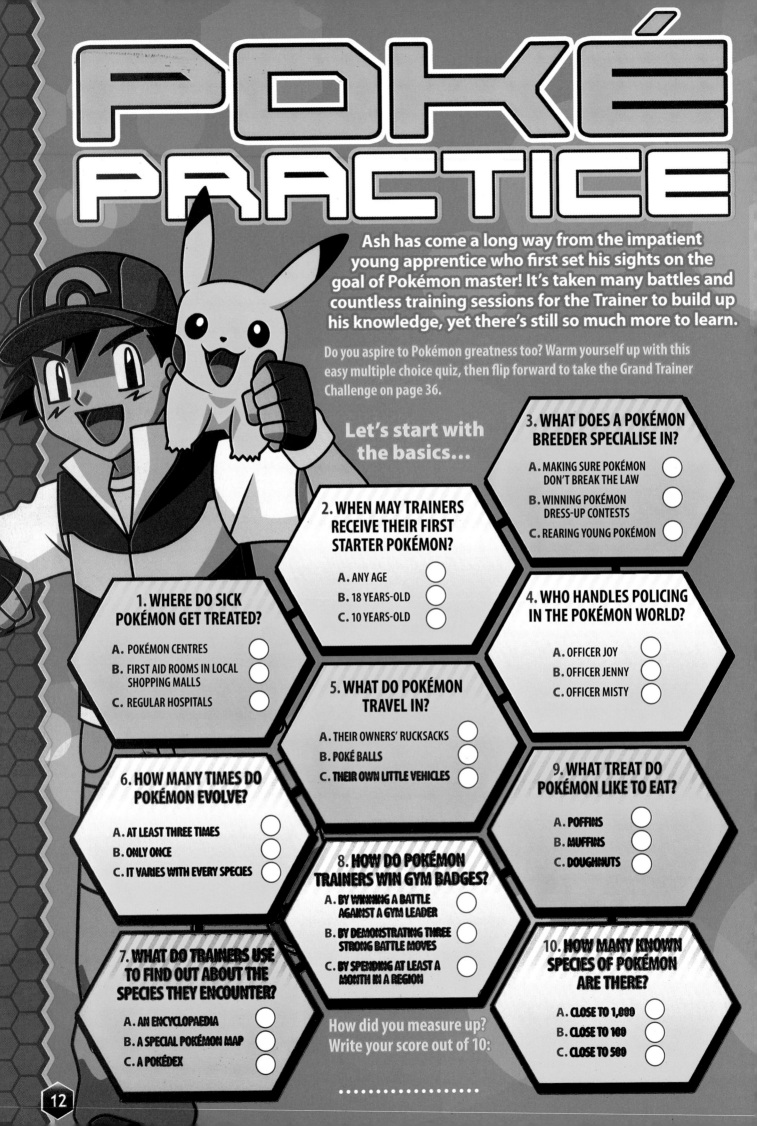

SMALL &
PERFECTLY FORMED

Pokémon come in all shapes and sizes! Here some of Sinnoh's smallest have been put under the spotlight. Colour each one in, then write its name underneath. If you get stuck, use the Sinnoh Pokédex pages to help you identify any tricky species.

1

2

4

3

TYPE TRIALS

Did you know that there are 17 different types of Pokémon? Each one has advantages over certain other types, and weaknesses too. See if you can recognise some of the different species groups that you might encounter in the Sinnoh region...

...THEN DRAW A LINE TO CONNECT EACH POKÉMON WITH ITS CORRECT TYPE...

A  WATER

B  ELECTRIC

C  ICE

D  GHOST

E NORMAL

F GRASS

1  MISDREAVUS

2 BUNEARY

3  FLOATZEL

4  CHERRIM

5  ELECTIVIRE

6  GLACEON

SINNOH WORD SEARCH

The Sinnoh region is an exotic blend of lush forest, lonely mountain ranges and turquoise lakes. Young Trainers will find many challenging Gyms there too – from Roark's Rock-specialist Oreburgh Gym to Volkner's Electric Gym Battle in Sunyshore City.

This letter grid is hiding the names of 10 Sinnoh locations. Study the squares closely, then draw a line through each and every one. Be vigilant! The words could be running in any direction, from diagonal to back-to-front.

T	M	I	R	O	N	I	S	L	A	N	D	D	U
W	E	X	J	O	X	I	T	M	V	X	K	E	T
I	S	N	O	W	P	O	I	N	T	C	I	T	Y
N	P	Z	O	W	E	D	Y	F	G	L	V	E	S
L	E	D	C	R	S	D	I	H	J	A	P	R	X
E	A	M	C	Q	O	J	V	O	L	K	R	N	K
A	R	G	B	J	K	C	M	K	P	E	K	A	R
F	P	A	W	B	F	K	T	I	H	V	P	C	A
T	I	R	H	T	Y	N	K	N	T	A	M	I	P
O	L	D	C	H	A	T	E	A	U	L	L	T	L
W	L	Q	R	J	B	P	G	K	H	O	A	Y	A
N	A	G	J	K	Q	H	M	A	D	R	M	M	P
T	R	O	P	H	Y	G	A	R	D	E	N	O	X

- SNOWPOINT CITY
- MOUNT CORONET
- PAL PARK
- TWINLEAF TOWN
- LAKE VALOR
- SPEAR PILLAR
- ETERNA CITY
- TROPHY GARDEN
- OLD CHATEAU
- IRON ISLAND

15

DEALING WITH DEFENSIVE TYPES!

Excitement fills the air as Ash's much anticipated Battle with Canalave Gym Leader Byron finally gets underway! Son Roark will referee, with Dawn and Brock nervously watching the action from the spectator gallery…

Ash took his place in the Gym Battle, Pikachu perching anxiously on his shoulder. Tension filled the air – the young Trainer was determined to show what he could really do!
"Hey Ash," waved Dawn. "Good luck."
There was no time to wave back, Roark was signalling for the contestants to get ready.
"The Gym Battle between Ash, the challenger," he announced, "… and Byron the Gym Leader will now start!"
Ash narrowed his eyes, concentrating on every word. "Both sides will use three Pokémon each and the Battle is over when all three of one side's Pokémon are unable to continue," explained Roark. "And in addition, only the challenger is allowed to substitute Pokémon!" Byron clapped his hands together in eager anticipation.

"I love fossils," bellowed the Gym Leader. "And I love defence!"
Ash thought hard. 'I know Byron's defence style's not going to make this easy, but there's no way that I'm going to lose this!'
Byron waved his spade, his cloak billowing behind him. He was a powerful presence and Ash knew that his experience was impressive too. "Just wait and see," shouted Ash. "I'll get that Mine Badge for sure!"
Byron chuckled, then flexed his awesome pecks. "That's the kind of spirit that I like, but this ain't gonna be a walk in the park I can tell you!" Roark waved his arms for silence. "Let the Battle begin!"

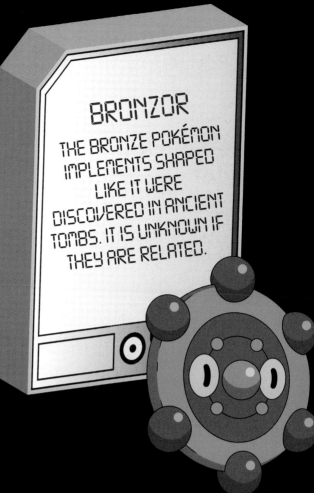

BRONZOR
THE BRONZE POKÉMON
IMPLEMENTS SHAPED
LIKE IT WERE
DISCOVERED IN ANCIENT
TOMBS. IT IS UNKNOWN IF
THEY ARE RELATED.

As soon as his son had stepped away from the arena, Bryon hurled his Poké Ball towards Ash. "Bronzor," he thundered. "Let's go!"

Dawn and Brock gasped as the disk-shaped warrior span into the Gym Battle. "Byron's spent countless hours intensively training that Pokémon," explained the pupil sat next to them.

Brock nodded. "It's gonna be a tough fight."

Ash looked up at his friends and grinned. "Knowing that Bronzor's a Steel and Psychic Type, there's no question that a Fire-Type's the best for this job," he reasoned. "Chimchar I choose you!"

Chimchar suddenly appeared, chattering with excitement. Roark stared at the Pokémon, then rubbed his eyes.

"I believe that I know that Chimchar," he cried, stepping forward for a closer look.

"Right!" nodded Ash. "He used to be Paul's not so long ago! But Chimchar's on my team now!"

The Pokémon eyed Bronzor, his flame flared in readiness.

Ash punched the air, willing his Pokémon forward. "Chimchar!" he commanded. "Flamethrower!" Chimchar's eyes narrowed as a torrent of burning heat blasted from its jaws, heading straight for Bronzor.

Byron signalled to his Pokémon, crying "Brace yourself!" Bronzor was soon engulfed in a beam of flames. Instead of retreating however, the Pokémon simply closed its eyes to withstand the blast. "Look!" said Dawn, leaping from her seat. "How can Bronzor handle Chimchar's Flamethrower?"

"Bronzor must have the ability Heatproof!" replied Brock. "That means that it can limit the damage from any Fire-Type that it encounters." Ash wasn't phased.

"We need more power," he urged. "Try Flamethrower one more time!"

Byron threw his head back and laughed. "Use that as much as you want!" he nodded. "Bronzor, Raindance!"

Bronzor suddenly angled itself up towards the opening in the arena roof. Light reflected off the Pokémon's body and within seconds clouds had begun to gather overhead.

Byron looked triumphant as a dark rain shower suddenly began to pour into the Gym, instantly extinguishing Chimchar's flames. "It's all part of Byron's strategy," confirmed Brock. "He's using a Water-Type move to throw Chimchar off its game!"

Pikachu leapt off Ash's shoulder, scampering forward to encourage his soaked team-mate. It was time for the Trainer to dig deep.

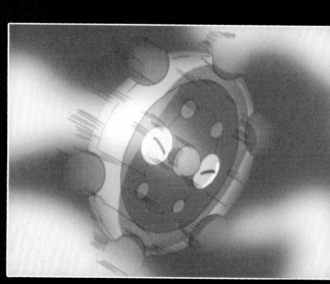

"Chimchar!" shouted Ash. "Use Dig, now!" At once the Pokémon rallied, diving down into the earth below the Gym Battle. Bronzor began to scan the ground, desperate to see where its opponent might surface.

"Dig is a defensive move," said Byron. "I'm impressed with Ash!"

When it heard Ash's signal, Chimchar leapt out of the ground, rushing forward to surprise Bronzor with another Flamethrower move. Byron's Pokémon was knocked backwards, but only for a moment.

"Dodge Bronzor," boomed Byron, warming up to the fight. "Then use Gyro Ball!" The spectators watched as Bronzor began to spin at super speed. Suddenly it was transformed into a fearsome rotating missile that was hurtling towards Chimchar!

"Awesome at attack and defence," admired Brock. "Just like a Gym Leader."

Ash countered with Flame Wheel, sending the Pokémon head-to-head. The Gym rocked as the pair collided in a massive crash, with both Chimchar and Bronzor sent reeling to the ground.

The spectators waited anxiously for one of the Pokémon to move. "Quick Chimchar!" begged Ash. "Stand up!"

"Show them what you're made of Bronzor" commanded Byron. Seconds seemed to pass like hours. Finally however, Chimchar staggered wearily to its feet. "Bronzor is unable to battle!" announced Roark. "Chimchar is the winner!"

Dawn clapped loudly, beaming with pride while Ash thanked his Pokémon, returning it to his Poké Ball. Byron turned to his Bronzor. "You didn't win, but it was a great battle thank you!"

"Don't start celebrating just yet Ash," grinned Roark. "Don't worry," nodded the Trainer. "I know that we're just getting going!"

While Ash battled his heart out, Team Rocket were snooping along the corridors of the Canalave Gym. The opportunity to go on an undisturbed fossil-stealing mission was too good to resist!

"Now da Twerp's out the way challenging Byron to a Battle, let's fulfil our fantasies with a flock of fossils!" grinned Meowth.
Jessie tossed her purple hair, her eyes shining wickedly. "We can give those fossils to the Boss," she trilled. "Then watch those Twerp heads take a loss!"

James stopped for a moment to peer through some double doors. "Oooh…" he murmured. Inside there was a huge kitchen , equipped with a giant fridge freezer.
Jessie pushed past him. "Even thieves get hungry!" she grinned. "Dat fridge's gotta be chockfull of grub!" agreed Meowth, following her in. Jessie threw open the fridge's doors. Every shelf was groaning with snacks!

"There are enough rations here to feed either a small city or the four of us!" squealed James. Meowth grabbed a handful of goodies. "Dis is what I call an icebox with class!"
"Let's eat!" yelled Jessie, stuffing food into her mouth. Suddenly the Team Rocket princess felt a tap on her shoulder. The trio turned round to see an Omayte, Omastar and a Kabuto – three formidable fossil Pokémon!

"Dey say that dis grub belongs to their pie-holes," groaned Meowth. "Not ours!"
"What are you going to do?" snapped Jessie, squaring up to the Pokémon. It was a silly question. Within moments Team Rocket found themselves blasting into the sky, with no food or fossils to show for it.

Back in the Gym, it was time for the second round of Ash and Byron's epic battle. "You made a good start," acknowledged Byron. "But I'm not finished yet!" Ash watched as the Gym Leader summoned Steelix from his Poké Ball.

"All right Buizel!" he replied. "I choose you!" "Byron's selected a Steel and Ground Type," Dawn observed. "As a Water-Type Buizel should have the advantage."

The pupil sitting next to the Co-ordinator shrugged his shoulders. "An advantage based on type doesn't always decide who the winner will be, that's for sure."

"True," agreed Brock. "But I figure that Ash probably knows that by now." The spectators watched closely, keen to see Ash's first move. Instead of leaping into action however, the Trainer stood motionless as if he were frozen to the spot.

"Getting the least little bit scared of my steely defence, Ash?" asked Byron.

Ash shook his head, trying to think on his feet.

He didn't want to risk another head-on attack that might come crashing back on his own Pokémon!

"Better get things movin'," resolved Ash. "Buizel, Water Gun, go!" Byron swiftly countered the Water-Type with Steelix's Screech move. The gush of water streaming from Buizel was suddenly blocked by a wall of sound. Brock leaned forward in his seat. "Steelix has blocked Buizel in its tracks!" he gasped. "That's what I call a defence!"

Ash and Pikachu both tried to get to Buizel, but the Screech move was far too powerful to block. Byron was on a roll.

"Great!" he shouted. "Now use Bind Steelix!" The Pokémon's enormous metallic tail uncoiled itself then plucked Buizel from the ground. The Water-Type was immediately trapped in Steelix's mighty grasp.

"Buizel!" cried Ash. "NO!"

Byron showed no mercy – he wanted to win this thing just as badly as Ash did! "Steelix!" he roared. "Let's finish this up with Iron Tail!" The gigantic Pokémon dropped Buizel onto the ground, then delivered a thundering blow with its tail. Ash's Water-Type was sent reeling into the sky, landing back on the floor with a dreadful thump.

Ash and his friends all shouted encouragement as Buizel tried and failed to get back on its feet. "Buizel can no longer battle!" confirmed Roark. "The win goes to Steelix!"

Ash wasn't listening. Instead he raced across the Gym to check that his Pokémon was all right. "Don't sweat it!" he smiled, as Buizel retreated to the Poké Ball. "You take a good rest."

Ash looked disappointed but undeterred as he waited for the next round to begin. "Now they each have two Pokémon left," said Brock, standing up to give his friend some encouragement. "It seems evenly matched." The pupil in the stand next to him seemed less hopeful for the newcomer. "Chimchar's already taken a bit of damage," he pointed out. "I think Byron's got the upper hand right now."

Dawn shook her head. She knew Ash well enough to be certain that he was no quitter! The Trainer had practised for this Battle for weeks – he wasn't going to let a few knocks hold him back.

"I tell you, you're wrong!" she insisted. "Ash is going to win it, I'm sure."

Boosted by his win, Byron didn't let up for one second.

"So Ash," he taunted. "How are you planning to take down my glorious Steelix?"

The young Trainer looked the Gym Leader square in the eyes. "I'm betting on Chimchar, that's how!"

Dawn and Brock gasped as the faithful Fire-Type re-entered the arena.

"It's got the advantage by type," admitted Brock. "But it still hasn't fully recovered from the last time." Chimchar bravely went in with Flamethrower, but everyone could see that his strength was diminished. Steelix towered over the Pokémon, then thrashed it into the air with its fearsome Iron Tail move.

"Dodge it!" urged Ash, gesturing for Chimchar to rescue a fall by using its Dig move.

Byron was pumped up with adrenalin.

"Make the earth tremble Steelix!"

Steelix batted Chimchar into the dirt time and time again. Brock, Dawn and Piplup watched in horror as their pal got overwhelmed by terrifying Steelix. Chimchar fought back valiantly, but it couldn't seem to make any headway against its awesome opponent.

"No flimsy defence is going to get past us!" announced Byron. "Use Bind!"

But instead of strangling its adversary, Steelix suddenly went crashing into the dust. There was a short, eerie silence.

"The battlefield must have been weakened by Chimchar using Dig," explained Brock.

Ash was quick to capitalise on the situation. Chimchar delivered a decisive Flame Wheel right between Steelix's eyes.

Roark called time, pronouncing Chimchar as the surprise winner.

"Awesome!" shouted Ash, punching the air with pride. "You did it!"

As the Gym Battle reached fever pitch, Team Rocket broke into the Canalave building one more time. The sneaky crew were determined not to blast off until they got their greedy hands on those fossils!

Jessie rubbed her hands as the trio tiptoed down the corridor. If she could get a big haul of fossils she knew that her boss Giovanni would reward her handsomely. Crime was about to start paying!

"Whassat!" hissed Meowth, holding a paw out to block them.

James and Jessie peered down the gloomy corridor. Something sinister was definitely making its way towards them!

"Crikey!" screeched James. "It a Kabutops!"

The gang started running in the other direction – the Kabutops began to flick its pincers menacingly.

"It must be doin' security for da Gym!" panicked Meowth, searching for the nearest getaway.

No one could hear Team Rocket's encounter from the Gym Battle. Everyone was waiting with baited breath to find out which Pokémon Byron would use next.

"I can see how you managed to win a badge from my son," conceded the Gym Leader. "But there's no way you're going to get past my Bastiodon!"

Dawn looked Byron's latest contestant up in her Pokédex.

BASTIODON
THE SHIELD POKÉMON
ANY FRONTAL ATTACK
IS REPULSED BY ITS
UNTRACTABLE IRON
HEAD ARMOUR.

"I knew that he'd save Bastiodon 'til last," whispered Ash. "Chimchar's gonna run out of steam soon!"

Pikachu leapt to the floor, its little arms waving furiously at the Rock-Steel Type.

"You're right Pikachu," nodded Ash. "We've gotta wrap this up fast!"

"Quick Chimchar!" yelled Ash, spurring his Pokémon forward. "Flamethrower, let's go!" Chimchar summoned all of its remaining power, channelling a jet of red-hot flames at Bastiodon. "Iron Defence!" countered Byron, brandishing his shovel. Bastiodon stood its ground, dipping its head like a shield. The flames licked and curled over the Pokémon, but nothing seemed to penetrate.

Byron stepped forward, urging Bastiodon to capitalise on his rock-hard defence. "Use Metal Burst!" he roared. "Now!" Suddenly Bastiodon's shield was engulfed by a dazzling forcefield that seemed to work like a mirror. Instead of simply repelling Chimchar's flames, Bastiodon was able to deflect them straight back at its rival!

Brock shook his head. "Bastiodon's using Metal Burst to return all the damage that it took from the attack." The beam of heat was too powerful even for plucky Chimchar to resist. Dawn held her head in her hands as the Pokémon connected with the blast. "You can do it Chimchar!" she cheered, hoping for a miracle.

Sadly it wasn't meant to be. Ash's Pokémon was sent tumbling to the ground, exhausted by the intense combat. "Chimchar is unable to battle!" called Roark. "Bastiodon is the winner!" "You did great," said Ash, helping the Pokémon over to the side of the arena. Even though it had lost its last duel, the young Trainer knew that Chimchar had given 110 per cent. Now it was time for the loyal Fire-Type to take it easy for a while.

Meanwhile, Team Rocket's escape from Kabutops had led the villains to the perfect hiding place.

"Dis must be where da fossils are kept!" smirked Meowth, looking round the darkened room.

"And since we found it we own it!" decided Jessie. Team Rocket were standing in a vast chamber crammed to the rafters with expensive fossils. They stared at the priceless exhibits, their faces twisted with greed.

"There are enough fossils in this room to necessitate renting an entire row of restorers," crooned James, wondering which ones to take first.

Suddenly Meowth came face to face with two massive Pokémon models.

"That's definitely an animated Armaldo," remarked James, looking pleased with himself. James eyed the green Pokémon with the purple-crested head. "And that must be a 3D Cradily!" Suddenly the Pokémon moved. The terrible twosome stepped back, realising that they'd made a horrible mistake.

"Thinkin' dey're fossils is silly!" moaned Meowth, as the very real Armaldo and Cradily prepared to attack.

"Silly us!" shouted the hapless Team. "We're blasting off again!"

"Time for my last Pokémon," said Ash, summoning all his courage. "Gliscor, I choose you!" The Ground-Flying Type swooped into the Gym, determined to put up a strong fight.

Dawn looked more unsure about Ash's choice. "If he wants to attack from above, wouldn't Staravia be better?" she asked, turning to Brock for advice.

The Breeder stayed calm.

"Ash chose Gliscor after carefully considering Bastiodon's moves," he answered. "This is Gliscor's first battle so we should expect great things." Ash gestured up to the Gym roof. The Trainer knew he had to do something radical to overcome Bastiodon's immovable shield.

"Up!" he commanded. "Then come at Bastiodon from behind with Steel Wing!"

Gliscor sky-rocketed up to the ceiling, then attacked its opponent using all its might.

"Use Iron Defence!" yelled Byron.

Even though it was slow and lumbering, Bastiodon easily turned on its heels. Gliscor's attacks were quickly repelled by the Pokémon's body armour.

"Time to shift from defence to offense!" grinned Byron. "Use Iron Head!"

Suddenly Bastiodon's whole body began to shine with a dazzling power surge.

"Get outta the way quick!" shouted Ash.

By now Bastiodon was running towards Gliscor, transformed into a living battering ram. Poor Gliscor was sent reeling across the Gym, struck by a massive body blow.

Things were looking desperate for Gliscor, but there was no way that Ash was going to give up. The Trainer thought carefully about his opponent, trying to find a weakness to exploit. "This is it Bastiodon!" decided Byron. "Use Flash Cannon!" The Pokémon came in to attack again, but this time his rival was ready for him.

"Gliscor, spread your wings an' dodge it!" urged Ash. The Pokémon swept out of Bastiodon's way just in time, swooping up towards the Gym roof. Within moments Gliscor was plummeting back down again, landing on its adversary's back.

"Awesome!" cried Ash. "Now use Fire Fang!"

Byron looked on in surprise as the tables started to turn. Gliscor leapt off Bastiodon's back only to use its tail to knock the great Pokémon off its feet. It took enormous effort, and there was a pause as the contestants tried to get their breath back.

'They're both running out of gas,' thought Ash. 'The next attack's going to decide the Battle!'

Byron was thinking the same thing. "Let's decide this match!" he roared, sending Bastiodon in with Flash Cannon.

Gliscor was ready for him. It countered with Sand Attack, throwing Bastiodon off its course. Ash and Pikachu punched the air.

"Let's finish this thing off with Fire Fang now!" The spectators looked on amazed as the Pokémon collided in one last showdown. The force of Gliscor's move was tremendous. With one final groan, Bastiodon fell to the ground. Roark stepped in to wrap up the match.

"Bastiodon is unable to battle and Gliscor is the winner," he announced. "The victory goes to Ash of Pallet Town!"

"All right Gliscor," beamed Ash. "We did it!"

Dawn and Brock rushed down to the arena floor to congratulate their friend.

"Great how you considered Byron's and your Pokémon's types and played up to Gliscor's strong points," said Brock, his face beaming with pride.

"Thanks Brock!" nodded Ash. "Not bad for your first Gym Battle Gliscor, not bad at all!" Gliscor looked battle weary, but it was grinning from ear-to-ear. When Ash praised it, the over-excited Pokémon swooped in for a hug, knocking the Trainer to the floor.

"That was so great!" gushed Dawn, her Piplup chirruping in agreement.
Ash laughed then got back on his feet. "In the end it all came down to Gliscor's fighting spirit."

A little later, the friends gathered outside the Canalave Gym.
"You sure worked hard," smiled Roark. "It's not easy to beat my dad!"

Ash grinned as Byron nodded in agreement. "Your Pokémon are so well trained too, congratulations," added the referee.
The gang watched as Byron solemnly stepped forward. "In recognition of you having broken through my perfect defence and toppling my prize Pokémon," he announced. "I hereby present you with the Mine Badge."

Byron handed Ash a case lined with red velvet. Inside, the shield-shaped prize sparkled in the warm light of the sunset.
"Thanks so much Byron!" replied Ash, totally awestruck by the honour.

The friends clapped as the young Trainer picked out the badge and held it to his chest. "Check it out," he whispered. "I got me a Mine Badge!"

It seems that the hard-fought battles are the most rewarding of all. The coveted Mine Badge will serve as a lasting reminder of just what rewarding Battling is all about as our Heroes' Sinnoh journey continues!

MATCH THE MOVES

Both Ash and Byron used an awesome selection of moves during their epic Battle! The Canalave Gym records seem to have got mixed up however. Can you unjumble the key moves that each Pokémon contestant used, writing the correct word beneath each one?

If this puzzle gets you scratching your head, flick back through the 'Dealing With Defensive Types' story starting on page 16.

ASH

CHIMCHAR
CORRECT MOVE
....

BUIZEL
CORRECT MOVE
....

GLISCOR
CORRECT MOVE
....

MOVES
- **WATER GUN**
- **STEEL WING**
- **FLAMETHROWER**

BYRON

BRONZOR
CORRECT MOVE
....

STEELIX
CORRECT MOVE
....

BASTIODON
CORRECT MOVE
....

MOVES
- **IRON TAIL**
- **RAIN DANCE**
- **METAL BURST**

ULTIMATE SINNOH POKÉDEX

This Sinnoh Pokédex is the bumper reference guide for Pokémon enthusiasts! Every Pokémon in the region is featured, providing the ultimate resource for would-be Trainers.

There are a staggering 224 fascinating species listed in this amazing guide. But one very famous Pokemon is missing! Study all of the pictures and facts about the creatures that roam the region and see if you can find who we deliberately left out! The answer is at the back of the book.

31

RAICHU

TYPE
ELECTRIC

WEIGHT
30.0kg

HEIGHT
0.8m

ABILITY
STATIC

CLEFAIRY

TYPE
NORMAL

WEIGHT
7.5kg

HEIGHT
0.6m

ABILITY
CUTE CHARM - MAGIC GUARD

CLEFABLE

TYPE
NORMAL

WEIGHT
40.0kg

HEIGHT
1.3m

ABILITY
CUTE CHARM - MAGIC GUARD

ZUBAT

TYPE
POISON-FLYING

WEIGHT
7.5kg

HEIGHT
0.8m

ABILITY
INNER FOCUS

GOLBAT

TYPE
POISON-FLYING

WEIGHT
55.0kg

HEIGHT
1.6m

ABILITY
INNER FOCUS

PSYDUCK

TYPE
WATER

WEIGHT
19.6kg

HEIGHT
0.8m

ABILITY
DAMP-CLOUD NINE

GOLDUCK

TYPE
WATER

WEIGHT
76.6kg

HEIGHT
1.7m

ABILITY
DAMP-CLOUD NINE

ABRA

TYPE
PSYCHIC

WEIGHT
19.5kg

HEIGHT
0.9m

ABILITY
INNER FOCUS - SYNCHRONISE

KADABRA

TYPE
PSYCHIC

WEIGHT
56.5kg

HEIGHT
1.3m

ABILITY
INNER FOCUS - SYNCHRONISE

ALAKAZAM

TYPE
PSYCHIC

WEIGHT
48.0kg

HEIGHT
1.5m

ABILITY
INNER FOCUS - SYNCHRONISE

MACHOP

TYPE
FIGHTING

WEIGHT
19.5kg

HEIGHT
0.8m

ABILITY
GUTS - NO GUARD

MACHOKE

TYPE
FIGHTING

WEIGHT
70.5kg

HEIGHT
1.5m

ABILITY
GUTS - NO GUARD

MACHAMP

TYPE
FIGHTING

WEIGHT
130.0kg

HEIGHT
1.6m

ABILITY
GUTS - NO GUARD

TENTACOOL

TYPE
WATER - POISON

WEIGHT
45.5kg

HEIGHT
0.9m

ABILITY
CLEAR BODY - LIQUID OOZ

TENTACRUEL

TYPE
WATER - POISON

WEIGHT
55.0kg

HEIGHT
1.6m

ABILITY
CLEAR BODY - LIQUID OOZE

GEODUDE

TYPE
ROCK - GROUND

WEIGHT
20.0kg

HEIGHT
0.4m

ABILITY
ROCK HEAD - STURDY

GRAVELER

TYPE
ROCK - GROUND

WEIGHT
105.0kg

HEIGHT
1.0m

ABILITY
ROCK HEAD - STURDY

GOLEM

TYPE
ROCK - GROUND

WEIGHT
300.0kg

HEIGHT
1.4m

ABILITY
ROCK HEAD - STURDY

PONYTA

TYPE	FIRE
WEIGHT	30.0kg
HEIGHT	1.0m
ABILITY	RUN AWAY - FLASH FIRE

RAPIDASH

TYPE	FIRE
WEIGHT	95.0kg
HEIGHT	1.7m
ABILITY	RUN AWAY - FLASH FIRE

MAGNEMITE
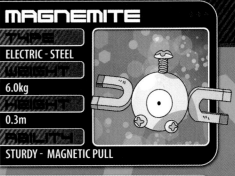

TYPE	ELECTRIC - STEEL
WEIGHT	6.0kg
HEIGHT	0.3m
ABILITY	STURDY - MAGNETIC PULL

MAGNETON

TYPE	ELECTRIC - STEEL
WEIGHT	60.0kg
HEIGHT	1.0m
ABILITY	STURDY - MAGNETIC PULL

GASTLY

TYPE	GHOST - POISON
WEIGHT	0.1kg
HEIGHT	1.3m
ABILITY	LEVITATE

HAUNTER

TYPE	GHOST - POISON
WEIGHT	0.1kg
HEIGHT	1.6m
ABILITY	LEVITATE

GENGAR

TYPE	GHOST - POISON
WEIGHT	40.5kg
HEIGHT	1.5m
ABILITY	LEVITATE

ONIX

TYPE	ROCK - GROUND
WEIGHT	210.0kg
HEIGHT	8.8m
ABILITY	ROCK HEAD - STURDY

LICKITUNG

TYPE	NORMAL
WEIGHT	65.5kg
HEIGHT	1.2m
ABILITY	OBLIVIOUS - OWN TEMPO

RHYHORN
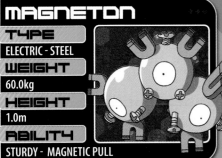

TYPE	GROUND - ROCK
WEIGHT	115.0kg
HEIGHT	1.0m
ABILITY	ROCK HEAD - LIGHTNING ROD

RHYDON

TYPE	GROUND - ROCK
WEIGHT	120.0kg
HEIGHT	1.9m
ABILITY	ROCK HEAD - LIGHTNING ROD

CHANSEY

TYPE	NORMAL
WEIGHT	34.6kg
HEIGHT	1.1m
ABILITY	NATURAL CURE - SERENE GRACE

TANGELA

TYPE	GRASS
WEIGHT	35.0kg
HEIGHT	1.0m
ABILITY	CHLOROPHYLL - LEAF GUARD

GOLDEEN

TYPE	WATER
WEIGHT	15.0kg
HEIGHT	0.6m
ABILITY	SWIFT SWIM - WATER VEIL

SEAKING

TYPE	WATER
WEIGHT	39.0kg
HEIGHT	1.3m
ABILITY	SWIFT SWIM - WATER VEIL

MR. MIME

TYPE	PSYCHIC
WEIGHT	54.5kg
HEIGHT	1.3m
ABILITY	SOUNDPROOF - FILTER

SCYTHER
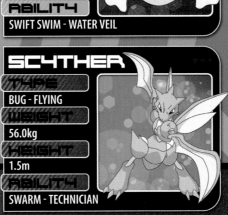

TYPE	BUG - FLYING
WEIGHT	56.0kg
HEIGHT	1.5m
ABILITY	SWARM - TECHNICIAN

ELECTABUZZ

TYPE	ELECTRIC
WEIGHT	30.0kg
HEIGHT	1.1m
ABILITY	STATIC

MAGMAR

TYPE	FIRE
WEIGHT	44.5kg
HEIGHT	1.3m
ABILITY	FLAME BODY

MAGIKARP

TYPE	WATER
WEIGHT	10.0kg
HEIGHT	0.9m
ABILITY	SWIFT SWIM

GYARADOS

TYPE	WATER FLYING
WEIGHT	235.0kg
HEIGHT	6.5m
ABILITY	INTIMIDATE

JOLTEON

TYPE	ELECTRIC
WEIGHT	24.5kg
HEIGHT	0.8m
ABILITY	VOLT ABSORB

EEVEE

TYPE	NORMAL
WEIGHT	6.5kg
HEIGHT	0.3m
ABILITY	RUN AWAY - ADAPTABILITY

VAPOREON

TYPE	WATER
WEIGHT	29.0kg
HEIGHT	1.0m
ABILITY	WATER ABSORB

FLAREON

TYPE	FIRE
WEIGHT	25.0kg
HEIGHT	0.9m
ABILITY	FLASH FIRE

PORYGON

TYPE	NORMAL
WEIGHT	36.5kg
HEIGHT	0.8m
ABILITY	TRACE - DOWNLOAD

SNORLAX

TYPE	NORMAL
WEIGHT	460.0kg
HEIGHT	2.1m
ABILITY	THICK FAT - IMMUNITY

HOOTHOOT

TYPE	NORMAL - FLYING
WEIGHT	21.2kg
HEIGHT	0.7m
ABILITY	KEEN EYE - INSOMNIA

NOCTOWL

TYPE	NORMAL - FLYING
WEIGHT	40.8kg
HEIGHT	1.6m
ABILITY	KEEN EYE - INSOMNIA

CROBAT

TYPE	POISON - FLYING
WEIGHT	75.0kg
HEIGHT	1.8m
ABILITY	INNER FOCUS

PICHU

TYPE	ELECTRIC
WEIGHT	2.0kg
HEIGHT	0.3m
ABILITY	STATIC

CLEFFA

TYPE	NORMAL
WEIGHT	3.0kg
HEIGHT	0.3m
ABILITY	CUTE CHARM - MAGIC GUARD

TOGEPI

TYPE	NORMAL
WEIGHT	1.5kg
HEIGHT	0.3m
ABILITY	HUSTLE - SERENE GRACE

TOGETIC

TYPE	NORMAL
WEIGHT	3.2kg
HEIGHT	0.6m
ABILITY	SERENE GRACE - HUSTLE

MARILL

TYPE	WATER
WEIGHT	8.5kg
HEIGHT	0.4m
ABILITY	THICK FAT - HUGE POWER

AZUMARILL

TYPE	WATER
WEIGHT	28.5kg
HEIGHT	0.8m
ABILITY	THICK FAT - HUGE POWER

SUDOWOODO

TYPE
ROCK

WEIGHT
38.0kg

HEIGHT
1.2m

ABILITY
ROCK HEAD - STURDY

AIPOM

TYPE
NORMAL

WEIGHT
11.5kg

HEIGHT
0.8m

ABILITY
RUN AWAY - PICK UP

YANMA

TYPE
BUG - FLYING

WEIGHT
38.0kg

HEIGHT
1.2m

ABILITY
COMPOUND EYES - SPEED BOOST

WOOPER

TYPE
WATER - GROUND

WEIGHT
8.5kg

HEIGHT
0.4m

ABILITY
DAMP - WATER ABSORB

QUAGSIRE

TYPE
WATER - GROUND

WEIGHT
75.0kg

HEIGHT
1.4m

ABILITY
DAMP - WATER ABSORB

ESPEON

TYPE
PSYCHIC

WEIGHT
26.5kg

HEIGHT
0.9m

ABILITY
SYNCHRONISE

UMBREON

TYPE
DARK

WEIGHT
27.0kg

HEIGHT
1.0m

ABILITY
SYNCHRONISE

MURKROW

TYPE
DARK - FLYING

WEIGHT
2.1kg

HEIGHT
0.5m

ABILITY
INSOMNIA - SUPER LUCK

MISDREAVUS

TYPE
GHOST

WEIGHT
1.0kg

HEIGHT
0.7m

ABILITY
LEVITATE

UNOWN

TYPE
PSYCHIC

WEIGHT
5.0kg

HEIGHT
0.5m

ABILITY
LEVITATE

GIRAFARIG

TYPE
NORMAL - PSYCHIC

WEIGHT
41.5kg

HEIGHT
1.5m

ABILITY
INNER FOCUS - EARLY BIRD

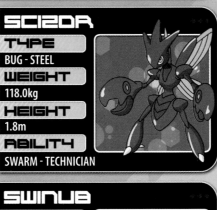

GLIGAR

TYPE
GROUND - FLYING

WEIGHT
64.8kg

HEIGHT
1.1m

ABILITY
SAND VEIL - HYPER CUTTER

STEELIX

TYPE
STEEL - GROUND

WEIGHT
400.0kg

HEIGHT
9.2m

ABILITY
ROCK HEAD - STURDY

SCIZOR

TYPE
BUG - STEEL

WEIGHT
118.0kg

HEIGHT
1.8m

ABILITY
SWARM - TECHNICIAN

HERACROSS

TYPE
BUG - FIGHTING

WEIGHT
54.0kg

HEIGHT
1.5m

ABILITY
SWARM - GUTS

SNEASEL

TYPE
DARK - ICE

WEIGHT
28.0kg

HEIGHT
0.9m

ABILITY
KEEN EYE - INNER FOCUS

SWINUB

TYPE
ICE - GROUND

WEIGHT
6.5kg

HEIGHT
0.4m

ABILITY
OBLIVIOUS - SNOW CLOAK

PILOSWINE

TYPE
ICE - GROUND

WEIGHT
55.8kg

HEIGHT
1.1m

ABILITY
OBLIVIOUS - SNOW CLOAK

CONTINUED PAGE 60

35

GRAND TRAINER

CHALLENGE

POKÉMON KNOWLEDGE

1 WHICH POKÉMON EVOLVES INTO MAGMORTAR?

....

2 UNSCRAMBLE THE LETTERS LAGGIR TO NAME THIS POKÉMON.

....

3 WHICH SINNOH POKÉMON HAS THE MOST EVOLUTIONS?

....

4 WHICH IS THE ODD ONE OUT BETWEEN GASTRODON, MANAPHY AND SHELLOS?

....

5 FILL IN THE MISSING LETTERS TO COMPLETE THIS ICE-TYPE'S NAME.

S _ _ R _ N _

6 WHAT IS THE MIDDLE EVOLUTION BETWEEN CLEFFA AND CLEFABLE?

....

7 WHAT TYPE OF POKÉMON IS MR. MIME?

....

8 WHICH POKÉMON LIKES TO SHARE ITS EGGS WITH INJURED PEOPLE?

....

PART 1 TOTAL

....

36

Do you have what it takes to become a true Pokémon master? Every year many thousands of young Trainers set out to follow in Ash Ketchum's footsteps – determined to collect cool Pokémon and win Gym Badges in every town they visit. Sadly only a handful show Ash's flair, determination and expertise.

Today Ash has thrown down a new gauntlet. There's space for a new Trainer in the Sinnoh League – are you good enough to make it? This is your chance to earn Pokémon glory for yourself! The questions will test you in four key areas:

1. Pokémon Knowledge
2. Observation
3. Combat Skills
4. Battle Gyms

PART 2
OBSERVATION

Study each close-up, then name the Pokémon that it belongs to.

Work your way through the quizzes, then check your level on page 39. **Good luck!**

1
....

2
....

3
....

4
....

5
....

6
....

7
....

8
....

PART 2
TOTAL
....

GRAND TRAINER CHALLENGE

COMBAT SKILLS

1 WHAT DOES LUCARIO USE TO PROTECT ITSELF?

....

2 WHAT DOES TOXICROAK SECRETE IN ITS KNUCKLE CLAWS?

....

3 GARDEVOIR WILL GUARD ITS TRAINER WITH ITS LIFE. TRUE OR FALSE?

....

4 WHAT IS PIPLUP'S SIGNATURE MOVE?

....

5 DOES HOUNDOUR TRACK ITS PREY ALONE OR IN A PACK?

....

6 WHAT BIRD-LIKE EVOLUTION OF STARAVIA WILL CHALLENGE FOES MUCH LARGER THAN ITSELF?

....

7  NAME THIS BOLD FIGHTING-TYPE POKÉMON.

....

8 TICK THE BATTLE MOVE THAT GLISCOR WOULD NOT USE?

FIRE FANG
STEEL WING
THUNDERBOLT

PART 3 TOTAL

....

PART 4
BATTLE GYMS

Read the details on each of these Sinnoh Gyms, then try and work out which badge each one presents to successful challengers. The names of the badges are listed below to help you.

BADGES: – ICICLE – COBBLE – MINE – FEN FOREST – RELIC – COAL – BEACON

1 GYM LEADER ROARK – OREBURGH CITY – ROCK

.... BADGE

2 GYM LEADER CANDICE – SNOWPOINT CITY – ICE

.... BADGE

3 GYM LEADER FANTINA – HEARTHOME CITY – GHOST

.... BADGE

4 GYM LEADER VOLKNER – SUNYSHORE CITY – ELECTRIC

.... BADGE

5 GYM LEADER MAYLENE – VEILSTONE CITY – FIGHTING

.... BADGE

6 GYM LEADER GARDENIA – ETERNA CITY – GRASS

.... BADGE

7 GYM LEADER BYRON – CANALAVE CITY – STEEL

.... BADGE

8 GYM LEADER CRASHER WAKE – PASTORIA CITY – WATER

.... BADGE

GRAND TOTAL

How well did you perform in the four parts of the Trainer Challenge? Turn to the answers at the back of the book, then give yourself a point for every question that you got correct.

1-8 BUDDING NOVICE
There's still a lot to learn, but your bright young mind is keen to absorb all there is to know about battling Pokémon. Keep on working then retake the test in a few weeks' time, you're bound to improve!

9-16 PROMISING APPRENTICE
You've got the right attitude for a promising young Trainer, you just need to build up your knowledge bank. Study the Pokédex pages and observe others in battle – you'll rise up through the rankings in no time!

17-14 TOP TRAINER
Your score is very impressive indeed, well done! You have a natural affinity with all Pokémon and the ambition to go far. Ash and Brock would be proud of such a respectable result, keep it up!

25-32 POTENTIAL POKÉMON MASTER
Very few people are gifted with the mental strength to get full marks in this challenge, congratulations! All of Sinnoh will be waiting to see how you use your skills in the future. Many triumphs lie ahead of you – enjoy them!

LEADING A STRAH!

Basking in the glow of Ash's sixth Badge win at the Canalave Gym, our Heroes are now headed to Chocovine Town, where Dawn's next Pokémon Contest is being held...

Brock checked his map, then led his pals down a pretty side street.

"The harbour should be just along here," he smiled, pointing to a small jetty lined with ferries.

Ash sprinted ahead to check out the departure board. The gang had to get going soon if they were going to make it to Chocovine Town in time for Dawn's Co-ordinator Contest!

"Wha...?" he cried. "The boats aren't running!"

Brock looked over his shoulder and frowned. "The boats are the fastest way to Chocovine Town."

Dawn's face fell – not making the Contest wasn't an option! She ran over to a passing business man, desperate to find out what was going on.

"It's because of them," replied the man, pointing to a flock of giant Wailord floating in the harbour. Ash peered across the water. The Pokémon were blocking the way to the open sea.

The Trainer flipped open his Pokédex.

WAILORD
THE FLOAT WHALE POKÉMON WAILORD CAN DIVE NEARLY 3,000 METRES ON ONE BREATH.

"Nobody's really sure why," added the businessman. "But those Wailord won't leave the harbour."

"They're the biggest of all Pokémon," said Brock. "Not easy to shift."

Ash scratched his head. "So the boats can't leave until they do, right?"

"Right," said the man. "And I can't tell you what a headache it is getting to work now."

Dawn's eyes filled with worry. "What do we do?"

"My belly thinks we should get some food," grinned Ash. "Then we can decide how we're gonna get there."

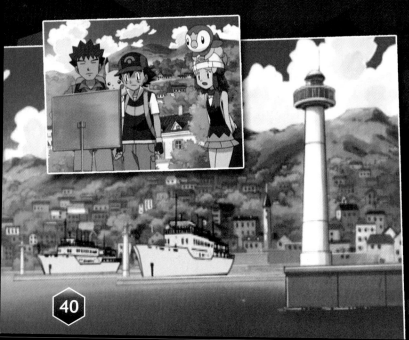

Brock found the perfect spot for the friends to take a break. The sun shone down as the Breeder brought out plate after plate of delicious delicacies.

"Lunch is served!" he announced proudly. "And here's my special Pokémon food for Pikachu and Piplup."

Brock held out a paper bag packed with goodies. Before it even made it to the table however, a Luxio appeared out of nowhere, snatching the Pokémon food out of Brock's hand!

"I know that Pokémon!" shouted Ash, opening his Pokédex.

Dawn gasped in surprise, but Piplup looked furious. The plucky Water-Type dashed towards the Luxio, determined to get its lunch back again. Luxio countered with a merciless blast of electricity. Poor Piplup reeled to the ground.

"You can't do that!" shouted Ash. "Pikachu, get Luxio!" Pikachu launched itself onto the Pokémon's back. In an attempt to throw Ash's friend off, Luxio began to violently shake its head. It lost its grip on the bag of Pokémon food, sending it spinning through the air.

"What's going on?" cried Dawn, as a Whismur and a Nidoran suddenly scuttled out of the undergrowth. The Whismur caught the bag of food, then ran after Luxio.

"Stop thieves!" bellowed Brock. "They're acting like some sort of team!"

Luxio and its buddies disappeared into the distance. Pikachu and Piplup dusted themselves down then gave chase – there was no way they were letting their lunch slip away that easily!

"Guys, no!" cried Ash and Dawn, following after.

41

In town, Team Rocket were breaking new ground – putting in an honest day's work at a building site! "Move a little earth and earn a little money," groaned Jessie, wiping the sweat from her brow. James grabbed his pickaxe and sighed. "With honest work and an empty tummy!" Meowth wandered across the site, pushing a wheelbarrow full of rocks.

"Nobody can say we've got rocks in our heads," he muttered, wondering when it was time to quit. Just then, Luxio, Whismur and Nidoran dashed past, closely followed by the irate Piplup and Pikachu. Jessie quickly spied Ash and his pals approaching too.

James' eyes lit up. The thought of doing some honest work had suddenly lost its appeal. "It's nice when primo Pokémon run right into our laps!" he grinned.

Jessie was on the same page as her purple-haired pal. "Especially when they're owned by Twerpish saps!"

Meowth scuttled forward and pressed a button on the side of the bulldozer parked up beside them. Suddenly the machine transformed itself into a giant robot – a terrifying addition to the Team. "Presentin da Oith – movin monsta' mashin' MECCA MAULA ONE!" cried Meowth.

"And it's primed for Pikachu!" sneered Jessie.

The mechanical menace began clawing at the concrete. Jessie, James and Meowth sat at the controls, guiding the robot forward. Ash arrived just in time to save Pikachu from its devastating claw. "Quick!" yelled the Trainer, diving down a manhole with Pikachu in his arms. Ash pulled the lid over the pair, then sat in the sewer below.

"Yeah!" cackled Meowth. "We eat manhole covers for lunch!"

Dawn gasped in horror as Team Rocket's bulldozing contraption began bashing the manhole with ground-shattering force. The cover was dented and bent, but luckily it didn't smash. James shouted in frustration. "We didn't bring a can opener!"

"Turn it loose, don't bend it!" screeched Jessie.

Dawn knew she had to do something – the manhole wasn't going to hold out forever! "Now Piplup!" she shouted. "Use Whirlpool!"

Piplup sprang into action, its little body whipping up a storm of water. The torrent of liquid spiralled round and round, sweeping up everything in its path.

"Brain drain!" shrieked Team Rocket. The hapless trio's bulldozer began to sink into the turbulent waters, but Piplup kept on going.

"Not annuda machine!" blurted Meowth as his invention bobbed into view for the last time. Team Rocket weren't far behind, overcome by the force of Piplup's attack. "You Twerps are so mean!" spat Jessie, as the trio were blasted out of town.

Ash reached for his Poké Ball – he needed to draft in some reinforcements! "All right Buizel," he cried. "I choose you!" Buizel dived into the canal and then began paddling towards a junction in the distance. "Can you find a way to get us outta here?" asked Ash.

Suddenly figures appeared way ahead of them. "It's those guys!" gasped the Trainer, recognising the Luxio, Whismur and Nidoran they'd been chasing earlier.

Before Ash could approach the Pokémon, Luxio lunged forward. A volley of lightning bolts whistled past Ash's ears. "We didn't do anything!" he shouted. "So what was that for?"

Buizel instantly leapt out of the water, counter-attacking Luxio with its awesome Aqua Jet move. There was a thunderous crash, but when the light cleared the Luxio and its friends had disappeared.

Once Team Rocket were safely out of the way, Dawn and Brock called down the manhole to make sure that Ash was OK.

Piplup scurried up to the metal plate and pulled with all its might. The dogged little Water-Type didn't stand a chance at lifting the lid, but Dawn felt proud of the effort.

"The manhole cover is so bent, I think this is going to be a problem," said Brock. No matter how hard he tugged, the lid wouldn't budge.

"It's OK guys!" shouted Ash. "Me and Pikachu will just have to find another way out!"
Ash looked around him. The Trainer was standing in a long, murky tunnel leading to a network of waterways. "I guess this canal must run underneath the whole town," he guessed. "We could get lost down here big time if we're not careful!"

Suddenly Ash and his Pokémon heard a low, moaning noise echoing from one of the waterways up ahead. The threesome followed the noise along the connecting tunnels, then peeped out from behind a corner.

"Did you hear that?" whispered Ash. "It's a Wailmer." The Wailmer was lying across the shadowy walkway, crying out in distress. Pikachu began to chatter in alarm – the Wailmer belonged in the water, not stranded on the side!
Ash's eyes widened as he spotted the Luxio approach and then start to feed the Wailer the Pokémon food that it had stolen from him earlier. "Luxio and his pals are just trying to take care of the big guy!" he guessed.

Ash didn't waste any more time, rushing forward to push Wailmer back into the water. At first the Luxio looked wary, but it stopped snarling when it realised what Ash was trying to do. The strangers worked together in a bid to get the Pokémon back into the canal, but the Wailmer's enormous body was just too big for them to budge.

WAILMER
THE BALL WHALE POKÉMON
IT SPOUTS WATER OUT OF ITS NOSE BUT BECOMES SLEEPY WHEN ITS BODY GETS DRY.

"That's it!" cheered Ash. "If we can get some water on the Wailmer, it will be able to roll itself back into the canal!"

Buizel opened its mouth wide, then sprayed the Pokémon with a steady jet of water. As if by magic, the Wailmer began to revive, quickly rolling itself back off the bank and into the underground waterway below.

"I wonder…" mused Ash. "Did you get separated from the group of Wailord that are hanging around in the harbour?"
The Wailmer dipped its head in agreement. Ash turned to Luxio, suddenly seeing the Pokémon in a whole new light.
"So you must be trying to lead the Wailmer back to where the rest of its buddies are," he gasped. "We gotta help out too!"

Bribery wasn't ideal, but it was the only option left. Dawn reached down to pick up a basket laden to the brim with tasty Pokémon poffins. Mamoswine stopped scratching as soon as it spotted the sweet treats.

"If you open the manhole cover," bargained Dawn. "You can have all these delicious poffins!" There was a deafening boom as the great twin tusk stamped its foot on the concrete. The manhole cover was sent spinning skyward. Unfortunately Dawn, Piplup and her poffins were too.

"Wow!" whistled Brock. "Just like a bottle cap!" There was a rush of air as the trio came crashing back towards the earth. Mamoswine opened its huge mouth to swallow the poffins, while Dawn braced herself for a nasty bump. Luckily it didn't come. Little Happiny wobbled left and right before catching Dawn and Piplup in its arms.

Back on the surface, Dawn and Brock were getting more and more frustrated. No matter what they tried, the bashed manhole cover was refusing to budge. "Not even Happiny can open it," shrugged Brock, watching the pink Pokémon close its eyes and heave.

Dawn sat on the kerb and thought hard. "I know!" she eventually cried. "Let's get Mamoswine to solve this!" The determined Co-ordinator spun her Poké Ball in the air, summoning the tusked Pokémon. Mamoswine was an impressive sight, its colossal bulk towering over the friends. "I want you to open the manhole cover," said Dawn, smiling sweetly.

The Pokémon turned its back on the young Co-ordinator. "Excuse me Mamoswine!" Dawn shouted. She stamped her foot in frustration. "Would you please listen to me for a change?" Mamoswine began to scratch its sizeable behind. Brock put his face in his hands – Dawn still had a lot of training to do with this Pokémon.

While Dawn and Brock were lowering themselves down into the town's sewer system, Ash was following Luxio deeper into the network of tunnels. Suddenly the group entered a large chamber with water on all sides.

"Zubat and Mothim!" whispered Ash, looking up to see flocks of the Pokémon hanging from the gloomy ceilings. A host of different Pokémon slowly started to emerge from the shadows. Prattling Teddiursa waved down from the rafters and dome-eyed Venonant scuttled out from the murky corners to greet them. Ash was amazed to see so many amazing species living together in such a lonely place! He turned to Luxio and grinned. "I get the feelin' that you're their leader, right?" The Electric-Type proudly showed its teeth. All around there was an atmosphere of total

harmony – fellow Pokémon all caring for each other. "So this totally explains why you would want to help the Wailmer that wandered in down here," added Ash, massively impressed.

A few tunnels along, Dawn and Brock were wondering which way to turn. Only Piplup seemed to know where it was going, scampering up the corridors then beckoning them forward with its wing.

"Are you sure that it's up here?" asked Brock, wishing that he had a map.

Piplup squawked in frustration and kept going. "Absolutely, positively certain?" added Dawn. The tunnel up ahead looked damp, dark and lonely. Ash and Pikachu couldn't really be up there, could they?

Now that Ash was one of the gang, Luxio didn't waste any more time. It led its new friend straight back out of the chamber, guiding him back down one of the narrow sewer tunnels. As he jogged to keep up, Ash noticed that the Wailmer was gliding along in the canal next to them. After a few minutes the group stopped in front of a huge underground weir.

"So you're telling me you fell all the way down from there?" asked the Trainer, pointing up to the gushing water. Wailmer nodded sadly.
"Getting back isn't going to be easy," reasoned Ash, wondering what he could do. Suddenly an idea popped into his head. Ash turned to Luxio. "We're gonna need some rope," he said. "As much as you can find!"

A few minutes' later the Wailmer was gripping the rope between its teeth. Ash and his pals were stationed at either end with the cord coiled around them. Buizel floated in the canal, ready to push the Wailmer on the Trainer's command. "Hold on tight, OK?" said Ash, wrapping the rope around his waist.

The Wailmer gripped the rope as hard as it could, then started to swim straight towards the tumbling weir. The tunnel echoed with the sound of gushing water as the team waited for their cue. "Now let's do it!" shouted Ash. "Everybody pull!" Ash and the Pokémon heaved, while Buizel used all its strength to push the Wailmer forward. With a massive splash the Pokémon sprang over the weir, into the canal above.

Ash cheered, then climbed the steps at the side of the weir. His heart sank. There ahead of them, was another weir with a drop five times as high! "You gotta be kidding me!" groaned the Trainer. "I don't think we'll be able to pull anything over that!"

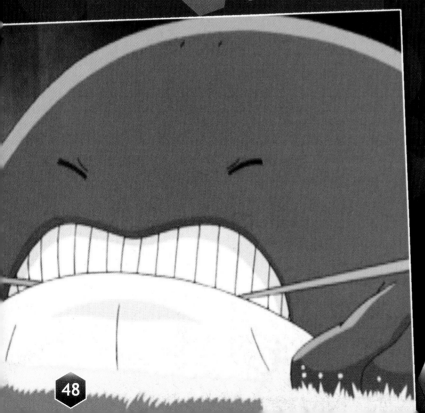

Ash peered up to the top of the weir. Luxio hung its head in disappointment, certain that they were beaten this time. It clearly didn't know the Trainer very well yet!

"Hey!" coaxed Ash. "I meant it when I told you that we'd get Wailmer back to his group."

Pikachu leant over his friend's shoulder then chattered something in his ear. Ash nodded, pointing back to the central chamber.

"We need to get the rest of your friends to help us Luxio," he urged. "Let's go!"

Way above the disappearing group, Dawn stepped onto the landing stage at the top of the weir. Piplup and Brock followed behind her, scouring the floor for a sign that Ash was nearby. "Are you sure we're going the right way?" Dawn asked, frowning at her Poké pal.
Piplup nodded its head, but looked as bewildered as she was. It glanced left and right, but didn't think to peer down.

Dawn wandered back down the corridor they'd arrived in, dismissing Piplup's directions once and for all.
"There's nobody here!" she decided.

As soon as they got back to Luxio's cavern, Ash addressed all the Pokémon living n the chamber. "I've got a plan to rescue the Wailmer," he revealed. "But you'll need to listen carefully, OK?" Rattata cautiously scampered over, followed by Nidoran and Teddiursa. Soon Ash and Pikachu were completely surrounded by willing volunteers.

Ash pointed at a group of Spheal that were bobbing in the water. "First Spheal will use their Ice Beam to freeze the canal all the way to the top!" he explained. "We're going to make a giant slide!" The Teddiursa clapped their hands when the Trainer told them to make a wooden sled out of their furniture. The idea was to place the Wailmer on the sled then use Luxio and Pikachu's electrical charge to blast the Pokémon up and over the icy weir. Ash grinned with pride. "Come on everybody, let's get to work!"

While the Teddiursa fetched their furniture, Ash began lashing it together with rope. Soon he had created an impressive sled large enough to bear Wilmer's impressive bulk. Once the sled was lowered into the correct position, the Spheal lined up in front of the weir.

The enthusiastic blue Pokémon channelled their Ice Beam move into the murky waters. Within seconds the sewer transformed into a polished sheet of ice. "Nice!" beamed Ash. "Now that's one frozen slide!" It took some effort to roll Wailmer on to the sledge, but with Buizel pushing from the back it finally made it.

Ash called everyone to attention. "It's time to roll!" The Spheal and Ash's Buizel gave the Wailmer a tremendous push, sending the sled skimming along the ice.

"All right Pikachu and Luxio, are you ready?" shouted Ash. "Give it as much power as you can!" The two Electric Pokémon both launched their impressive Iron Tail move. The sparks kick-started the sledge, buzzing it forwards at super speed. The Wailmer held on for its life as the platform shooted further up the glistening slide.

Crack! Ash raised his hands to his head as the rope began to snap with Wailmer's weight. Luxio and Pikachu struck again just in time. The sled was sent gliding through the air, finally touching down at the top of the weir.

"Yay!" roared Ash. They've really done it!

Ash and his team began to celebrate just as Dawn, Brock and Piplup stumbled back into the waterway. Dawn looked at Piplup sheepishly – it had been right after all! Ash quickly filled his pals in about what he'd been up to.

"I'll bet the Wailmer in the harbour have been worrying about the missing Wailord," said Dawn, thinking things through.

Dawn smiled. "Everything's going to be alright. Look! The exit's up ahead."

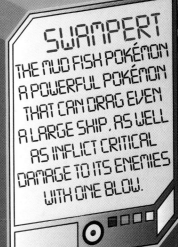

SWAMPERT
THE MUD FISH POKÉMON
A POWERFUL POKÉMON THAT CAN DRAG EVEN A LARGE SHIP, AS WELL AS INFLICT CRITICAL DAMAGE TO ITS ENEMIES WITH ONE BLOW.

But before the friends could lead the Wailmer to safety, another obstacle blocked their path. A very tense Swampert lurched itself out of the canal, blasting the Heroes with thick sewer mud. "Uh-oh," groaned Brock. "Looks like we're in the middle of Swampert's territory and it's on the attack!"

Ash wracked his brains, trying to find the right Pokémon to deal with a Ground-Type like this. Finally he settled on Grotle.

"OK!" he instructed. "Use Razor Leaf!"
Grotle bombarded Swampert with a barrage of barbed leaves. The Mud Fish Pokémon winced at the attack before finally slinking back into the water. Ash didn't like fighting wild Pokémon, but sometimes it was unavoidable.

"Sorry about that," he called, leading Wailmer out towards the light.

While Ash ran down to han[d]
Dawn and Brock found their w[ay]
control centre. Brock had spot[ted]
was trapped by a drawbridge, [and]
work out how to lift it up.

Once Swampert had been s[eparated from the]
sewers, Ash tore into the bridg[e]
The gang found the right butto[n but it wouldn't]
operate without a key!

"Go Pikachu!" he cried, pointing [at the]
circuit board. The plucky Poké[mon sent a bolt]
of electricity fizzing into the bo[ard. The]
bridge opened slightly.

"That worked!" shouted Broc[k. "But we]
need more power!"

Luxio leapt to Pikachu's aid, clos[ely followed]
by Dawn's Pachirisu. The voltage[s]
snowballed as the Pokémon cha[nnelled power]
into the drawbridge. After a few [more]
seconds, the bridge finally open[ed.]

The gang ran out of the tunnel, emerging on the banks of the harbour. Ash, Dawn and Brock squinted in the sunlight.

"Finally!" grinned Ash. "It's great to be outside again!"

Wailmer gurgled happily as it swam out to the open water. "You go and join your friends now," smiled Dawn. The Pokémon had only swum a few metres when something amazing happened. Wailmer began to swell and glow from the top of its blowhole right down to the tip of its tail! Brock beamed – their new friend was evolving into a Wailord right before their eyes!

He turned to Ash and Dawn only to see horror etched across their faces. "It's too big to fit under the bridge now," gasped Dawn.

Ash pointed to another shape skimming through the water. "It's Swampert!" he yelled. "He's coming back for more!

The friends cheered to see the drawbridge raise itself up, clearing a path for the new Wailord. All the sewer Pokémon scampered out of the tunnel, keen to see it safely on its way.

"It opened," cooed Ash. "Time to get movin' Wailord." The gigantic Whale Pokémon ploughed through the water, making a safe passage to its family. As it joined the pod, all of the Wailord sprayed a sheen of water into the air. A stunning rainbow suddenly began to glisten above their heads. "Maybe that's their way of thanking us for helping them," suggested Dawn.

Ash turned to Luxio and smiled.
"I'm never going to forget any of you guys as long as I live!" he promised.
The Luxio nuzzled the young Trainer, sending a playful spark into his shoulder.

"Hey," laughed Ash. "You're welcome if that was a 'thank you'!"

Brock got to his feet, then looked up at the afternoon sky.
"I guess we ought to get back on the road now," he said.

"Right!" beamed Ash. 'But my stomach says we oughta take a little break at the Pokémon Centre, ya know?"

Dawn raised her eyes and chuckled. "When it comes to your stomach, missing lunch is a no-no!"
"No," agreed Ash. "I mean – yeah!"

No matter what size or shape, our Heroes will help any Pokémon they can – in this case leaving a grateful Wailord, Luxio and many friends in their wake!

SPARKY SPOTS

All of Luxio's evolutions are pretty impressive! This group of Shinx, Luxio and Luxray have gathered at a remote Sinnoh breeding ground. Take a close look at the Electric-Types as they snarl and prowl. There are only two identical pictures of Luxray to be found – can you circle them both with a colourful felt-tipped pen?

MURKY MAZE

Ash has located Luxio, Dawn and Brock want to be reunited with him too. Help the friends find the right path through the underground tunnels. Step with care – the gloomy corridors are crammed with dead-ends and blocked passageways.

MISSING LINKS

Study these Pokémon evolution chains then write in the missing stage to complete each one. The missing Pokémon you need to choose from are all shown along the bottom of the page.

1. LICKILICKY

2 ....

3. TENTACOOL

4. PICHU

5 ....

6. TURTWIG

....

HAUNTER

....

....

TANGROWTH

GROTLE

GENGAR

RAICHU

....

PIKACHU

TORTERRA

GASTLY

TANGELA

TENTACRUEL

LICKITUNG

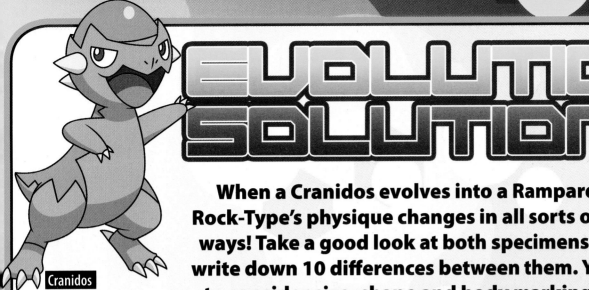

EVOLUTION SOLUTIONS

Cranidos

When a Cranidos evolves into a Rampardos, the Rock-Type's physique changes in all sorts of amazing ways! Take a good look at both specimens and then write down 10 differences between them. You'll need to consider size, shape and body markings to fully understand the evolution that has taken place.

Rampardos has...

1. ....
2. ....
3. ....
4. ....
5. ....
6. ....
7. ....
8. ....
9. ....
10. ....

Got it cracked? Now jot down two core similarities between the species known as the Head Butt Pokémon.

Cranidos and Rampardos have...

1. ....
2. ....

Rampardos

Gible has an impressive set of teeth! The Dragon-Ground Type hides itself for hours inside caves, leaping out to pounce on passing prey. Why not draw your own sketch of the snappy Pokémon?

Copy the lines in each of the small Hexagons into the corresponding blank panel on the bigger grid.

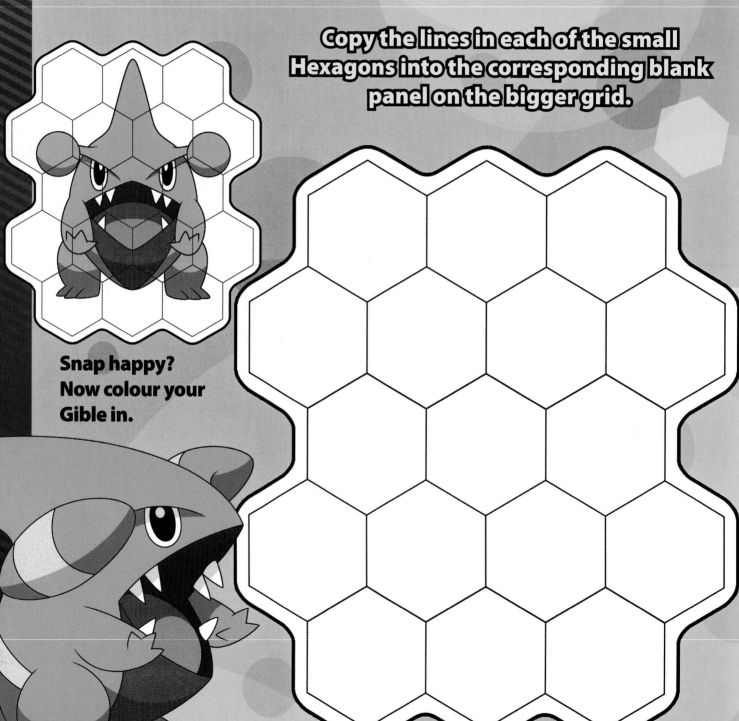

Snap happy?
Now colour your
Gible in.

SHY SHADOWS

Some timid Pokémon prefer to keep themselves hidden from view! Study the shadowy outlines of these shy types, then write their names underneath.

??????????? ??????????? ???????????

??????????? ??????????? ???????????

Can't shine a light on things? These jumbled Pokémon names should point you in the right direction...

FROSLASS UMBREON ABRA
TOGEKISS BUNEARY PILOSWINE

REMORAID

TYPE
WATER

WEIGHT
12.0kg

HEIGHT
0.6m

ABILITY
SNIPER - HUSTLE

OCTILLERY

TYPE
WATER

WEIGHT
28.5kg

HEIGHT
0.9m

ABILITY
SNIPER - SUCTION CUPS

MANTINE

TYPE
WATER - FLYING

WEIGHT
220.0kg

HEIGHT
2.1m

ABILITY
WATER ABSORB - SWIFT SWIM

HOUNDOUR

TYPE
DARK - FIRE

WEIGHT
10.8kg

HEIGHT
0.6m

ABILITY
FLASH FIRE - EARLY BIRD

HOUNDOOM

TYPE
DARK - FIRE

WEIGHT
35.0kg

HEIGHT
1.4m

ABILITY
FLASH FIRE - EARLY BIRD

PORYGON 2

TYPE
NORMAL

WEIGHT
32.5kg

HEIGHT
0.6m

ABILITY
TRACE - DOWNLOAD

ELEKID

TYPE
ELECTRIC

WEIGHT
23.5kg

HEIGHT
0.6m

ABILITY
STATIC

MAGBY

TYPE
FIRE

WEIGHT
21.4kg

HEIGHT
0.7m

ABILITY
FLAME BODY

BLISSEY

TYPE
NORMAL

WEIGHT
46.8kg

HEIGHT
1.5m

ABILITY
NATURAL CURE - SERENE GRACE

WURMPLE

TYPE
BUG

WEIGHT
3.6kg

HEIGHT
0.3m

ABILITY
SHIELD DUST

SILCOON

TYPE
BUG

WEIGHT
10.0kg

HEIGHT
0.6m

ABILITY
SHED SKIN

BEAUTIFLY

TYPE
BUG - FLYING

WEIGHT
28.4kg

HEIGHT
1.0m

ABILITY
SWARM

CASCOON

TYPE
BUG

WEIGHT
11.5kg

HEIGHT
0.7m

ABILITY
SHED SKIN

DUSTOX

TYPE
BUG - POISON

WEIGHT
31.6kg

HEIGHT
1.2m

ABILITY
SHIELD DUST

WINGULL

TYPE
WATER - FLYING

WEIGHT
9.5kg

HEIGHT
0.6m

ABILITY
KEEN EYE

PELIPPER

TYPE
WATER - FLYING

WEIGHT
28.0kg

HEIGHT
1.2m

ABILITY
KEEN EYE

RALTS

TYPE
PSYCHIC

WEIGHT
6.6kg

HEIGHT
0.4m

ABILITY
SYNCHRONISE - TRACE

KIRLIA

TYPE
PSYCHIC

WEIGHT
20.2kg

HEIGHT
0.8m

ABILITY
SYNCHRONISE - TRACE

GARDEVOIR

TYPE
PSYCHIC
WEIGHT
48.4kg
HEIGHT
1.6m
ABILITY
SYNCHRONISE - TRACE

AZURILL
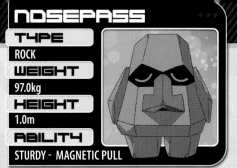
TYPE
NORMAL
WEIGHT
2.0kg
HEIGHT
0.2m
ABILITY
THICK FAT - HUGE POWER

NOSEPASS
TYPE
ROCK
WEIGHT
97.0kg
HEIGHT
1.0m
ABILITY
STURDY - MAGNETIC PULL

MEDITITE

TYPE
FIGHTING - PSYCHIC
WEIGHT
11.2kg
HEIGHT
0.6m
ABILITY
PURE POWER

MEDICHAM

TYPE
FIGHTING - PSYCHIC
WEIGHT
31.5kg
HEIGHT
1.3m
ABILITY
PURE POWER

ROSELIA

TYPE
GRASS - POISON
WEIGHT
2.0kg
HEIGHT
0.3m
ABILITY
NATURAL CURE - POISON POINT

SWABLU

TYPE
NORMAL - FLYING
WEIGHT
1.2kg
HEIGHT
0.4m
ABILITY
NATURAL CURE

ALTARIA

TYPE
DRAGON - FLYING
WEIGHT
20.6kg
HEIGHT
1.1m
ABILITY
NATURAL CURE

BARBOACH

TYPE
WATER - GROUND
WEIGHT
1.9kg
HEIGHT
0.4m
ABILITY
OBLIVIOUS - ANTICIPATION

WHISCASH
TYPE
WATER - GROUND
WEIGHT
23.6kg
HEIGHT
0.9m
ABILITY
OBLIVIOUS - ANTICIPATION

FEEBAS

TYPE
WATER
WEIGHT
7.4kg
HEIGHT
0.6m
ABILITY
SWIFT SWIM

MILOTIC

TYPE
WATER
WEIGHT
162.0kg
HEIGHT
6.2m
ABILITY
MARVEL SCALE

DUSKULL

TYPE
GHOST
WEIGHT
15.0kg
HEIGHT
0.8m
ABILITY
LEVITATE

DUSCLOPS

TYPE
GHOST
WEIGHT
30.6kg
HEIGHT
1.6m
ABILITY
PRESSURE

TROPIUS

TYPE
GRASS - FLYING
WEIGHT
100.0kg
HEIGHT
2.0m
ABILITY
CHLOROPHYLL - SOLAR POWER

CHIMECHO
TYPE
PSYCHIC
WEIGHT
1.0kg
HEIGHT
0.6m
ABILITY
LEVITATE

ABSOL
TYPE
DARK
WEIGHT
47.0kg
HEIGHT
1.2m
ABILITY
PRESSURE - SUPER LUCK

SNORUNT
TYPE
ICE
WEIGHT
16.8kg
HEIGHT
0.7m
ABILITY
INNER FOCUS - ICE BODY

CONTINUED PAGE 82

DRAW YOUR
DREAM TEAM

Ash firmly believes that all Pokémon should be treated with kindness and respect. His theory seems to work – many species choose to follow the Trainer instead of being captured in a Poké Ball.

Which three Pokémon would you choose to take on your travels? Each one that you select needs to be able to bring something special to your battles! Flick through the Pokédex pages, then draw the species you like best in here.

DON'T FORGET TO COLOUR THE PAGE IN WHEN YOU'VE FINISHED SKETCHING!

HEADS YOU WIN

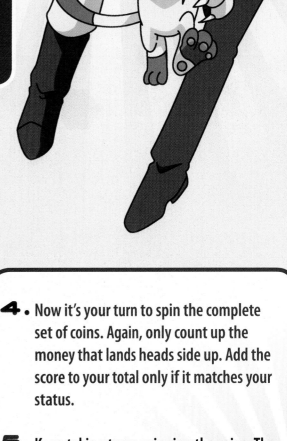

When Team Rocket aren't thinking about their bellies, they've got their minds on money. The sneaky cheats are happy to beg, borrow and steal loot from anywhere they can!

Here's a cool money game that will drive villains like Jessie, James and Meowth to distraction! Challenge a friend to a match then find out which of you really has the golden touch!

WHAT YOU WILL NEED

- PAPER AND PENCILS -
- ONE SET OF COINS STARTING FROM ONE PENNY AND GOING UP TO A 50 PENCE PIECE -
- A BIT OF LUCK! -

HOW TO PLAY

1. Choose one of you to be an 'even' player and the other to be 'odd'.

2. Ask your opponent to spin all the coins, watching them until they lay flat on the table. The player should only pick up the coins that land heads side up.

3. Ask your friend to count up the value of the coins in his hand. If the amount matches their status as 'odd' or 'even' they score the value of the coins. If the amount is different, they score nothing.

4. Now it's your turn to spin the complete set of coins. Again, only count up the money that lands heads side up. Add the score to your total only if it matches your status.

5. Keep taking turns spinning the coins. The winner is the player who reaches £5 first!

THE POKÉMON A TO Z

Do you have a favourite Pokémon for every letter of the alphabet? See if you can write a description or draw a picture in all of the letter boxes below. A few have been filled in already to get you started!

A...is for Arceus
A legend of Sinnoh mythology, it is said to have shaped the universe.

B...

C...

D...

E...

F...

G...is for Giratina
Giratina takes on two forms depending on the world it inhabits.

H...

I...is for Infernape This Fire-Fighting Type attacks using a special kind of martial art.

J...

K...

L...

M...

N...

O... is for Onix, this fearsome Rock Snake Pokémon can bore through rocky ground far below the surface.

P...

Q... is for Quagsire Quagsire can be found lying at the bottom of river beds, waiting for prey to stray into its mouth. It is a sluggish Pokémon.

R...

S...

T...

U...

V... is for Vaporeon One of Eevee's seven evolutions, Vaporeon has adapted itself so that it is perfectly suited to aquatic life.

W...

X...

Y...

Z...

One of the last three letters doesn't have a Pokémon in the Sinnoh region – which is it?

TOP TIP

Use the Pokédex pages to help you if you get stuck!

65

Steeling Peace of Mind!

Now that the harbour is clear, our Heroes are waiting to make the trip by boat to Chocovine Town – the site of Dawn's next Pokémon Contest. Meanwhile over on Iron Island, their friend Barry is squaring up to his own unexpected challenge…

Barry was having a fantastic workout with his elite Pokémon – Heracross and Empoleon. "Heracross!" bellowed the ambitious Trainer. "Use Megahorn!"

The rocky terrain of Iron Island rumbled as Heracross executed the move perfectly. Empoleon stamped its foot, eager to show what it was capable of too.

Barry pointed to the sky. "Use Hydro Canon, now!" There was a deafening gush as Empoleon amassed a swirling pool of water. Suddenly a super-powered jet blasted across the horizon, annihilating anything in its path.

"You two are looking great," nodded Barry. "With our combined power we could challenge and beat any Gym!" Empoleon returned to its friend's side, its steely eyes flashing with the exertion.

Suddenly a purple spark began to crackle across Empoleon's body. The Pokémon's beak contorted as if it were wracked with pain.

Barry was immediately concerned. "What's the matter?" he asked, looking to see what was wrong. Before Barry could take another step, Empoleon lunged forward. Its awesome wings beat up and down with a fury that the young Trainer had never seen before. "Hey Empoleon," gasped Barry, ducking for cover behind a rock. "What's gotten into you?" Empoleon wasn't listening. Instead the possessed Pokémon began to pelt Barry and Heracross with its unrelenting jet stream.

Over at the harbour, Dawn was getting excited about her impending Contest. She and her friends chatted happily in the sunshine while they waited for the ferry to arrive.

"Ash," asked the Co-ordinator. "Have you decided which Gym you're going to challenge next?" Ash proudly waved his map, pointing to a city not far from Chocovine Town.

"I've set my sights on the Snowpoint Gym," he answered.

"We were thinking about heading north to Snowpoint City after your Contest is over," explained Brock.

Dawn hugged Piplup to her chest. "Sounds great!" she cooed. "I've never been there before!"

It was time for the friends to go down to the pier when Nurse Joy ran over to meet the group. "Sorry Ash," she cried. "You have a phone call."

Ash and his friends whizzed round to Nurse Joy's Pokémon Centre and flicked on the flat screen. A picture of their friend Barry appeared.

"So Ash," he crooned, full of bravado. "Manage to win at the Canalave Gym?"

Ash pulled out his Mine Badge and waved it at the camera. "You bet I did!"

"All right!" smirked Barry. "I guess I'll have to treat you as a true rival now. You should feel honoured." The Trainer's bragging didn't last long -- when Ash asked him about his Pokémon Barry's face fell.

"Something's really wrong with Empoleon," he sighed. "All of a sudden he doesn't even recognise me!" Barry pointed to the clinic behind him. Ash and his friends saw Empoleon lying in a medical chamber, being treated by a Nurse Joy and her Chansey. "Empoleon's not the only one acting strange," continued Barry. "Bunches of other Pokémon all over the island have gone crazy too!"

Ash and his pals piled onto the Iron Island ferry the moment that it opened for boarding. The boat set off precisely on time, which was lucky for Ash. The plucky Trainer was itching with impatience – all he wanted to do was get there and get the problem cracked!

"Can't this thing go any faster?" he groaned, peering across the deck.

"I wish you would calm down," sighed Dawn. "You sound just like Barry!"

While the friends tried to pass the time, Team Rocket lurked unseen in the waters below. The half-baked crime team didn't have a clue why Ash's travel plans had changed, but they were determined to tag along and find out.

"Wherever they go, we go!" vowed Jessie.

"The Twerps must have business there," guessed James, hoping for an opportunity to snatch Ash's Pikachu. Meowth set their course for Iron Island – it was time for some serious snooping!

Barry described the havoc that was devastating the island. Herds of Steelix, Geodude and other native Pokémon were rampaging night and day, attacking the landscape and each other!

"Nurse Joy can't work out what's wrong either," sighed Barry. "I guess I'll just have to figure this thing out myself."

Ash didn't have to think twice – he couldn't bear to hear about Pokémon being in trouble!

"You know we'll come over there and help you out!" he cried, turning to Dawn. "Right?"

Even though her Contest was looming, Dawn didn't hesitate to offer her support.

"The next ferry to Iron Island leaves in 15 minutes," said Brock. "We'll be with you in no time."

Barry's face filled with emotion.

"We'll be together before ya know it!" promised Ash.

As soon as the ferry docked on Iron Island, Ash, Brock and Dawn hurried over to the Pokémon Centre. Nurse Joy showed them in to the reception area and then checked her register. It appeared that Barry had already left.
"I don't believe it!" Ash spluttered. "He's gone?" The astonished Trainer turned to his friends. There was just no helping some people!

"I'm sorry," said Nurse Joy. "He insisted that he had to go. He wouldn't listen!"

"We should have known that Barry would do something like this," replied Dawn.

Brock was too distracted to comment. He was lost in the deep blue pools of Nurse Joy's pretty eyes. "Hearing you apologise causes me great pain…" he began, trying to woo the fair lady. Brock's Croagunk delivered a sharp blow with

his toxic fingers. The Breeder's courtship ended right there!

When Ash asked to see Barry's Empoleon Nurse Joy's face fell.
"It's still under treatment," she sighed, showing the visitors into a bay filled with medical chambers. "I haven't been able to work out why only the Steel-Type Pokémon are being affected!" Dawn looked across at the patients. Dozens of Pokémon were lying in rows, their faces twisted with pain. "The poor things," she gasped, desperate to help somehow.
Ash thanked Nurse Joy, then led the team towards the door. It was time to find out what was up with Iron Island.

LAIRON
IT SMASHES ITS STEELY BODY AGAINST OTHERS TO FIGHT OVER TERRITORY.

Ash, Brock and Dawn hiked for hours into the heart of the Island – a lonely terrain covered with dark granite outcrops.

"I hope that Barry's OK," whispered Dawn. It certainly was a barren and unwelcoming kind of place! Little brown Diglett popped their heads out of the ground, twitching with nervous energy. Suddenly a terrifying white Pokémon studded with spines thundered out of the rocks.

"It's a Lairon!" shouted Ash. Dawn started to tremble. "The Diglett must be trying to get away from it!" It soon became clear that the Lairon wasn't after the Mole Pokémon. The tortured Steel-Rock Type rampaged through the rubble, violently shaking its head.

"It must be trying to block out all of its intense pain," explained Brock.

Ash didn't care about the risks, he was going in! "We gotta try and help!" he bellowed. "Let's go Pikachu!"

Dawn and Brock cried out with worry as the Electric-Type tried to floor Lairon with its Thunderbolt move. The attack was hopeless – Lairon was trapped in its own private torment. Pikachu's volts smashed against its body, but it didn't seem to feel a thing.

"Lairon's hurt," observed Brock. "But for some reason it seems unfazed by the pain!" "Watch out!" shrieked Dawn, as Lairon came crashing back towards Ash. Pikachu pushed its best friend out of the way just in the nick of time. "That was close," gasped Ash. "Thanks pal!"

Suddenly an even more terrifying threat loomed onto the horizon. An out-of-control Metang crashed through the cliff, driving a flock of frenzied Steel-Types before it. The island was plunged into chaos as Geodude, Skarmory and Gravelers thundered in all directions.

"It's like they're trying to hurt themselves!" shouted Ash, wondering how to calm the pandemonium.

"Awful!" agreed Dawn. "I can't believe this!" Brock's eyebrows knitted with worry. "I'd like to know what's going on."

Pikachu impulsively dragged Ash back towards the mountainside, just as furious Aggron pushed its way through the bedrock up ahead. The troubled Pokémon roared in anguish, obliterating rocks as if they were made of powder. Without a thought for his own safety, Ash flung himself into Aggron's path.

"Stop it!" he barked. "Why are you trying to destroy the island?"

Dawn turned white with fear – this was madness! "Come back Ash," she begged. "Please!" The young Trainer waved his arms in a desperate bid for Aggron's attention. "You've gotta stop all this right now!"

Ash's shouting had an effect, but not the one that he had anticipated. Aggron opened its jaws and blasted the ground in a furious display of power.

Dawn covered her eyes, certain that Ash was in grave danger.

Aggron attacked again, but this time its aim was more accurate. Before it could blast Ash into pieces, a tall stranger swept in and gathered the young Trainer in his arms. The stranger leapt to safety just as the spot that Ash had been standing on was obliterated completely.

Ash was astonished by his mystery rescuer. The man carried the young Trainer to the edge of the rocky clearing and then muttered instructions to a muscular Lucario.

"Use Close Combat," he ordered, glancing back at Aggron.

Lucario didn't hesitate. The loyal Pokémon began to pummel Aggron in the jaw, dodging its blasts with an unrivalled speed. A short battle ensued, but the Lucario sent Aggron crashing to the ground in a matter of moments.

"Are you alright?" asked the stranger. Ash pulled himself together fast. "Sure," he replied. "But that was really something!"

The man smiled. "It was a close call certainly."

Dawn and Brock scuttled over to their friend, the relief on their faces clear to see. The man gestured to a fork in the path that twisted off to the left. While the shaken friends walked away from the devastation, Lucario climbed to the top of the highest outcrop.

"What's it doing?" asked Dawn. "Scanning the area with its aura," answered the man. He exchanged glances with the Pokémon, then briefly nodded his head. "Apparently the area is safe. How about taking a break?" While the group sank to the ground, Ash checked Lucario out in his Pokédex.

LUCARIO
IT HAS THE ABILITY TO SENSE THE AURAS OF THINGS. IT UNDERSTANDS HUMAN SPEECH.

Dawn, Brock and Ash were relieved to sit down for a while.

"Thanks a whole lot for saving me before!" beamed Ash. "Nice ta meet ya!"

The man tipped his hat in greeting.

"Hi! My name is Riley," he replied. "I specialise in Steel-Types." Dawn remembered their eventful morning. There certainly were a lot of Steel Pokémon on Iron Island!

"The rocky terrain here is the perfect homeland for me," Riley explained. "But it is currently in danger!"

Ash immediately looked concerned, wondering if this trouble could be connected to Barry in some way.

"Lucario and I are trying to get to the bottom of these strange occurrences," added Riley, his face deadly serious.

"But isn't Lucario a Steel-Type too?" asked Dawn.

"Yes, but it's a Steel-Type and a Fighting-Type," said Riley. "It's surrounding itself with its protective aura!"

The friends looked across to Lucario. The strong Pokémon nodded its head in calm acknowledgement. When Ash looked more closely, he was just able to detect a soft blue glow emanating from Lucario's body. The aura wrapped itself around Lucario like a suit of armour.

"That is so cool!" whistled the budding Trainer.

"What a great defence," agreed Dawn.

"We've actually come to the island looking for someone," said Brock. "He's a boy named Barry." Riley tried to think.

"Barry?" he replied earnestly. "I'm afraid that I haven't seen him…"

Unbeknown to Ash and his friends, Barry wasn't so far away after all. While they were speaking with Riley, the stressed-out Trainer was tearing across the rocks with his Heracross in tow. A clutch of sparking Magnemite jostled and crashed behind them. Barry didn't dare think what their combined voltage might be!

"We have to jump Heracross!" shouted Barry, spotting the end of the road looming up ahead. The duo launched themselves off the rocky platform, but the drop was much deeper than Barry anticipated. Just as he thought his Training time was up, Heracross lifted him up and beat its wings.

"Phew!" he cried. "Thanks a lot!"
Unfortunately the pals weren't out of trouble yet. A frenzied Skarmory suddenly darted out of the sky, blasting Heracross with a direct hit. Barry and the Bug-Type tumbled to the ground.

"Woah!" cried Barry, wondering who or what had broken his fall.

A rather battered Jessie lifted her head out from underneath the crash site.
"Of all the lame-brained landings that has got to be the worst!" she hissed, dusting herself down. Barry gasped as Meowth and James crawled out from underneath her.
"Oh no!" he yelped. "Not you!"
Team Rocket were equally dismayed by the chance meeting. The characters sprang apart at once.
"Our problem has been Twerps from day one!" spat James, squaring up for a fight.

Barry didn't wait to take the first knock.
"Heracross!" he roared. "Fury Attack now!"
The Pokémon and Team Rocket clashed, but the match was far too even. Both sides soon found themselves sitting back on their behinds, wondering what to do next.

While Barry was working out how to shake off Team Rocket, Riley shared what he knew about the recent happenings.

"Lucario and I have discovered that there's a special low frequency sound wave covering the island," he explained. "It only affects Steel-Type Pokémon."

Ash looked confused. "Low frequency?"

"That's why their senses and demeanour have been altered," nodded Riley.

"And that's why they don't feel any pain?" guessed Brock.

The pieces were slowly starting to fall into place, but Ash didn't like it at all. "The way they're slamming their bodies into rocks and hurting themselves they must be takin' some serious damage!" he frowned. Riley told Brock how he was working on uncovering the source of the wave and then stopped at a barren crossroads.

"This path will lead you back into town," he smiled. "If I do happen to run into Barry I'll tell him to meet you there." Ash shook his head. The impulsive youngster wasn't going anywhere until this was wrapped up! Deep down Ash knew that the key to helping Barry had something to do with the mysterious sound wave that Riley had been talking about. "We wanna go with you!" he protested. Riley didn't give in easy. "It's too dangerous," he replied. "Sorry."

"All of us want to help," insisted Brock. "We're all Trainers," begged Dawn. "We have to." Riley and Lucario looked unsure. Both knew that tricky decisions lay ahead.

"Will you hesitate to attack a Pokémon that's gone berserk?" challenged Riley.

Dawn felt torn. "That won't be easy."

"Perhaps," conceded Riley. "But if you hesitate and get defeated you won't be able to save those truly in need!"

It couldn't have been a better time for Ash to join forces with Riley – Barry needed his help more than ever. Team Rocket stood scowling in front of him, their faces full of malice.

"I get it now," he suddenly exclaimed. "You're the ones who caused the Steel-Types to go crazy! I'm fining you all!"

Jessie looked unimpressed. "I never carry cash." Meowth and James rolled their eyes, this time they were actually innocent!

"We may be crooks," admitted Meowth. "But we do have a heart."

Barry found himself distracted. He could hear a machine whirring and banging at the top of the crag above them.

"That must be your contraption, correct?" he snapped in an accusing tone. Jessie, James and Meowth were genuinely bewildered. Wild with anger, Barry marched the hapless trio up the mountainside to examine the evidence.

The trio gasped when they saw the red-haired tyrant below. Mars from Team Galactic stood with her hands on her hips, presiding over a curious gold machine in a domed case. Golbat flapped around her, while a vicious Purugly prowled at her side.

"Isn't that girl one of you guys?" asked Barry. Jessie sniffed. "In your dreams Twerp!" Meowth's kitty eyes flamed. After their disastrous encounter in Celestic Town, now was their chance to take their revenge on Mars and her crew.

"We've got the element of surprise on our side," plotted James. "What they don't know will hurt them." Sadly there was little time to be smug. Before Meowth could even think of hatching a plot, Barry, Heracross and Team Rocket found themselves batted down into the quarry below. The unlikely associates landed in a pile at Mars' feet.

Mars looked very amused by her unexpected guests. "If it isn't Team Rocket," she snarled. "I'd love to chat, but I'm a bit busy right now." The evil mistress lifted one hand in the air, but didn't bother to look up. A snapping flock of Golbat immediately prepared to dive-bomb Barry and his cohorts.

Heracross leapt to his friend's defence, but it was soon bitten into submission.

"How dare you do that to my Pokémon," cried Barry, opening his Poké Ball so that the Bug-Type could retreat and lick its wounds. Suddenly Carnivine and Seviper appeared, leaping to Heracross's defence. Barry was stunned to realise that Team Rocket had sprung to his aid!

"Don't hold your Twerpish breath," scowled Jessie. "We have a bone to pick with these fashion freaks."

While Lucario was beginning to pick up the source of the sound wave, Barry and Team Rocket were battling for survival. Mars pummelled the visitors with her most aggressive Pokémon, outnumbering them three to one.

"Come on!" shouted Jessie. "It's time to hit back!"

"Time for my Fury Swipe!" hissed Meowth, flicking out its razor sharp claws.

Mars pointed at Purugly, roaring "Counter with your Fury Swipe!"

The catfight got nasty, but Team Galactic always had the upper hand. Barry and Team Rocket were driven back and back until they fell into a deep pit on the edge of Mars' lair. James sulked, struggling to get his breath. "We were routed in record time!"

While Team Rocket squabbled and passed the blame for their latest disaster. Barry took a look around him. The group were sitting in the depths of a gloomy canyon, but he could see some familiar figures carved into the walls. The Trainer gulped nervously, wondering why there was a giant effigy of Dialga and Palkia looming above them…

Mars couldn't resist jeering down at her captives. "Would you mind staying down there for a while?" she sneered in mock politeness. "You're a major eyesore!"

While Team Rocket railed again their prison-keeper, Barry began to feel more and more nervous. Something big and probably dangerous was going on down here!

Just then, a servant distracted Mars from her taunting. "Excuse me," she said. "We're now ready for the final stage." The flame-haired leader threw her head back and laughed.

"I'll have to leave you to it," she grinned, heading away from the mouth of the pit. Jessie was furious. "You come back there this instant!"

"We're not done with you yet!" added Meowth.

"Don't worry," Barry whispered under his breath. "I'll get myself out of here even if it's the last thing I do!" Fortunately help, or at least a friendly face, was nearly at hand. Riley, Ash, Dawn and Brock had finally found their way to Team Galactic's base.

"It looks like some kind of ancient shrine!" whispered Ash, leaning down for a closer look.

"It means this place might have something to do with the Sinnoh legend…" replied Brock. "…and Team Galactic!"

Riley looked confused. "Who are they?"

"An organisation who are trying to uncover the secret of time and space," muttered the Breeder. "Apparently they're going after Dialga and Palkia."

"The low frequency sound that was causing all the trouble has to be coming off these ruins," gasped Riley. "This has to be the source."

The friends watched the people amongst the rocks below. The shrine was hewn out of a strange metal-like substance that none of them had ever seen before.

"I'll bet that Team Galactic found the shrine and dug it up," said Dawn.

Riley's face looked deathly serious. "No doubt about it."

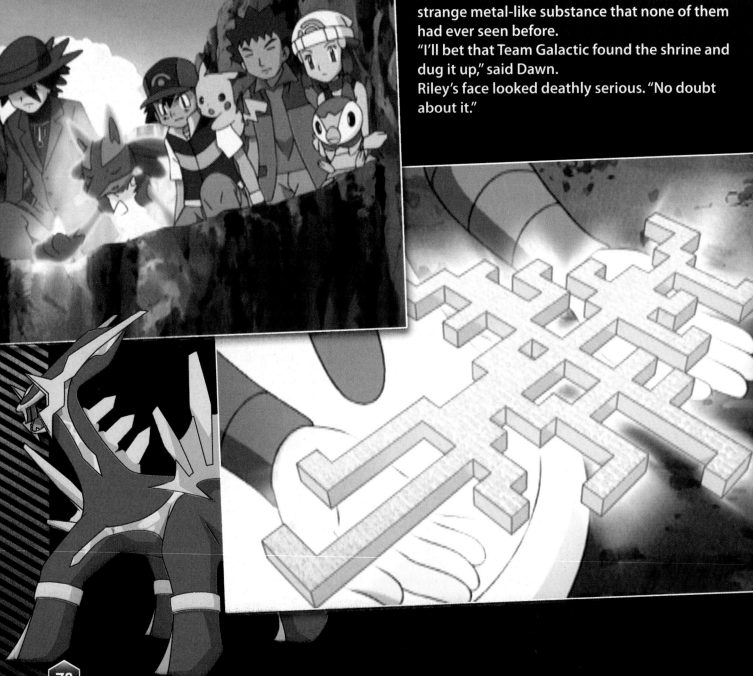

There was a hushed silence as Mars lifted a complex golden key from the heart of the machine. Dawn, Ash and Brock watched as she walked solemnly towards the ancient ruins, fitting the key into a hole in the metal wall. Riley held his breath– the key fitted exactly!

Suddenly the two great carvings of Dialga and Palkia lit up, glowing in the darkness above Barry and Team Rocket. The legendary Pokémon seemed to come to life, a prehistoric power emanating from their very likenesses.

"Perfect!" cried Mars. "Just like Cyrus said!" Way above the ancient effigies, Lucario began to tremble with the force of events.

"You must be sensing great power," whispered Riley. "Focus your aura and find out as much as you can!"

Just then a blinding light flashed from each of the carvings, meeting at a point above the golden key.

Mars and her cronies shielded their eyes as a white beam seared its way up a ruined obelisk in front of them, channelling into the sky above Iron Island. Its intensity was so powerful, everyone had to shield their eyes.

Ash squinted into the air. The beam was going across the Sinnoh skies, straight towards the far crest of Mount Coronet way off on the mainland. He turned to tell Riley, but something in Lucario's eye held him back. The normally tranquil Pokémon was staring at the group with a look of pure menace.

"What is it?" asked Riley, trying to grip its arm. Ash held him back. "Careful!" he warned. "Lucario's acting strange."

Suddenly the Pokémon began to shake with an intense rage just like the other Steel-Types they'd witnessed earlier. The power of Team Galactic's light beam must have pierced Lucario's aura! "No!" cried Riley. "Not you too?"

Ash and his friends got ready to defend themselves from imminent attack.

Once again our Heroes have crossed paths with the evil Team Galactic! What could they be after now and how can they be defeated?

Continued on Page 88...

MAKE YOUR OWN...

POKÉMON DOOR SIGN!

With this cool bedroom door sign, you can make it clear to your friends and families where your allegiance lies! All you need are some basic art supplies and a bit of imagination.

You will need:

- An old cardboard box with no printing on
- Scissors
- Ruler
- Pencil
- Old newspapers
- Poster paints
- Brush
- PVA glue

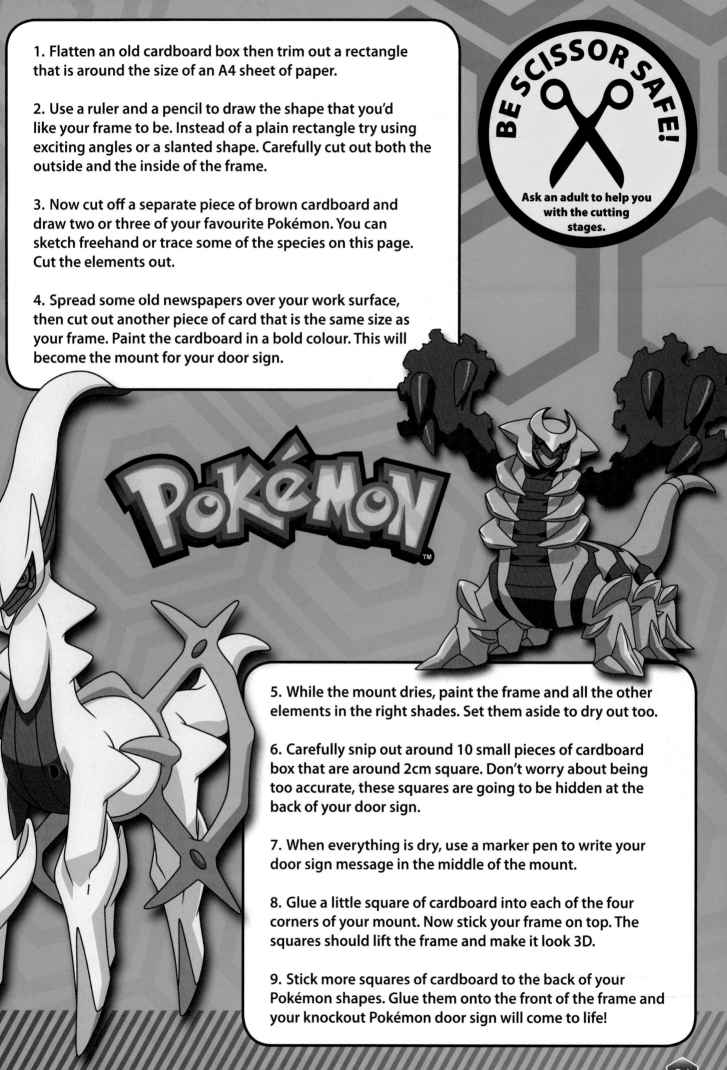

1. Flatten an old cardboard box then trim out a rectangle that is around the size of an A4 sheet of paper.

2. Use a ruler and a pencil to draw the shape that you'd like your frame to be. Instead of a plain rectangle try using exciting angles or a slanted shape. Carefully cut out both the outside and the inside of the frame.

3. Now cut off a separate piece of brown cardboard and draw two or three of your favourite Pokémon. You can sketch freehand or trace some of the species on this page. Cut the elements out.

4. Spread some old newspapers over your work surface, then cut out another piece of card that is the same size as your frame. Paint the cardboard in a bold colour. This will become the mount for your door sign.

BE SCISSOR SAFE!

Ask an adult to help you with the cutting stages.

5. While the mount dries, paint the frame and all the other elements in the right shades. Set them aside to dry out too.

6. Carefully snip out around 10 small pieces of cardboard box that are around 2cm square. Don't worry about being too accurate, these squares are going to be hidden at the back of your door sign.

7. When everything is dry, use a marker pen to write your door sign message in the middle of the mount.

8. Glue a little square of cardboard into each of the four corners of your mount. Now stick your frame on top. The squares should lift the frame and make it look 3D.

9. Stick more squares of cardboard to the back of your Pokémon shapes. Glue them onto the front of the frame and your knockout Pokémon door sign will come to life!

GLALIE

TYPE
ICE

WEIGHT
256.5kg

HEIGHT
1.5m

ABILITY
INNER FOCUS - ICE BODY

TURTWIG

TYPE
GRASS

WEIGHT
10.2kg

HEIGHT
0.4m

ABILITY
OVERGROW

GROTLE

TYPE
GRASS

WEIGHT
97.0kg

HEIGHT
1.1m

ABILITY
OVERGROW

TORTERRA

TYPE
GRASS - GROUND

WEIGHT
310.0kg

HEIGHT
2.2m

ABILITY
OVERGROW

CHIMCHAR

TYPE
FIRE

WEIGHT
6.2kg

HEIGHT
0.5m

ABILITY
BLAZE

MONFERNO

TYPE
FIRE - FIGHTING

WEIGHT
22.0kg

HEIGHT
0.9m

ABILITY
BLAZE

INFERNAPE

TYPE
FIRE - FIGHTING

WEIGHT
55.0kg

HEIGHT
1.2m

ABILITY
BLAZE

PIPLUP

TYPE
WATER

WEIGHT
5.2kg

HEIGHT
0.4m

ABILITY
TORRENT

PRINPLUP

TYPE
WATER

WEIGHT
23.0kg

HEIGHT
0.8m

ABILITY
TORRENT

EMPOLEON

TYPE
WATER - STEEL

WEIGHT
84.5kg

HEIGHT
1.7m

ABILITY
TORRENT

STARLY

TYPE
NORMAL - FLYING

WEIGHT
2.0kg

HEIGHT
0.3m

ABILITY
KEEN EYE

STARAVIA

TYPE
NORMAL - FLYING

WEIGHT
15.5kg

HEIGHT
0.6m

ABILITY
INTIMIDATE

STARAPTOR

TYPE
NORMAL - FLYING

WEIGHT
24.9kg

HEIGHT
1.2m

ABILITY
INTIMIDATE

BIDOOF

TYPE
NORMAL

WEIGHT
20.0kg

HEIGHT
0.5m

ABILITY
SIMPLE - UNAWARE

BIBAREL

TYPE
NORMAL - WATER

WEIGHT
31.5kg

HEIGHT
1.0m

ABILITY
SIMPLE - UNAWARE

KRICKETOT

TYPE
BUG

WEIGHT
2.2kg

HEIGHT
0.3m

ABILITY
SHED SKIN

KRICKETUNE

TYPE
BUG

WEIGHT
25.5kg

HEIGHT
1.0m

ABILITY
SWARM

SHINX

TYPE
ELECTRIC

WEIGHT
9.5kg

HEIGHT
0.5m

ABILITY
INTIMIDATE - RIVALRY

LUXIO
TYPE
ELECTRIC
WEIGHT
30.5kg
HEIGHT
0.9m
ABILITY
INTIMATE - RIVALRY

LUXRAY
TYPE
ELECTRIC
WEIGHT
42.0kg
HEIGHT
1.4m
ABILITY
INTIMATE - RIVALRY

BUDEW
TYPE
GRASS - POISON
WEIGHT
1.2kg
HEIGHT
0.2m
ABILITY
POISON POINT - NAUTURAL CURE

ROSEADE
TYPE
GRASS - POISON
WEIGHT
14.5kg
HEIGHT
0.9m
ABILITY
POISON POINT - NATURAL CURE

CRANIDOS
TYPE
ROCK
WEIGHT
31.5kg
HEIGHT
0.9m
ABILITY
MOULD BREAKER

RAMPARDS
TYPE
ROCK
WEIGHT
102.5kg
HEIGHT
1.6m
ABILITY
MOULD BREAKER

SHEILDON
TYPE
ROCK - STEEL
WEIGHT
57.0kg
HEIGHT
0.5m
ABILITY
STURDY

BASTIDDON
TYPE
ROCK - STEEL
WEIGHT
149.5kg
HEIGHT
1.3m
ABILITY
STURDY

BURMY — PLANT CLOAK
TYPE
BUG
WEIGHT
3.4kg
HEIGHT
0.2m
ABILITY
SHED SKIN

BURMY — SANDY CLOAK
TYPE
BUG
WEIGHT
3.4kg
HEIGHT
0.2m
ABILITY
SHED SKIN

BURMY — TRASH CLOAK
TYPE
BUG
WEIGHT
3.4kg
HEIGHT
0.2m
ABILITY
SHED SKIN

WORMADAM — PLANT CLOAK
TYPE
BUG - GRASS
WEIGHT
6.5kg
HEIGHT
0.5m
ABILITY
ANTICIPATION

WORMADAM — SANDY CLOAK
TYPE
BUG - GRASS
WEIGHT
6.5kg
HEIGHT
0.5m
ABILITY
ANTICIPATION

WORMADAM — TRASH CLOAK
TYPE
BUG - GRASS
WEIGHT
6.5kg
HEIGHT
0.5m
ABILITY
ANTICIPATION

MOTHIM
TYPE
BUG - FLYING
WEIGHT
23.3kg
HEIGHT
0.9m
ABILITY
SWARM

COMBEE
TYPE
BUG - FLYING
WEIGHT
5.5kg
HEIGHT
0.3m
ABILITY
HONEY GATHER
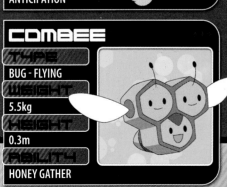

VESPIQUEN
TYPE
BUG - FLYING
WEIGHT
38.5kg
HEIGHT
1.2m
ABILITY
PRESSURE

PACHIRISU
TYPE
ELECTRIC
WEIGHT
3.9kg
HEIGHT
0.4m
ABILITY
RUN AWAY - PICK UP

BUIZEL
TYPE	WATER
WEIGHT	29.5kg
HEIGHT	0.7m
ABILITY	SWIFT SWIM

FLOATZEL
TYPE	WATER
WEIGHT	33.5kg
HEIGHT	1.1m
ABILITY	SWIFT SWIM

CHERUBI
TYPE	GRASS
WEIGHT	3.3kg
HEIGHT	0.4m
ABILITY	CHLOROPHYLL

CHERRIM
TYPE	GRASS
WEIGHT	9.3kg
HEIGHT	0.5m
ABILITY	FLOWER GIFT

SHELLOS EAST
TYPE	WATER
WEIGHT	6.3kg
HEIGHT	0.3m
ABILITY	STICKY HOLD - STORM DRAIN

SHELLOS WEST
TYPE	WATER
WEIGHT	6.3kg
HEIGHT	0.3m
ABILITY	STICKY HOLD - STORM DRAIN

GASTRODON EAST
TYPE	WATER - GROUND
WEIGHT	29.9kg
HEIGHT	0.9m
ABILITY	STICKY HOLD - STORM DRAIN

GASTRODON WEST
TYPE	WATER - GROUND
WEIGHT	29.9kg
HEIGHT	0.9m
ABILITY	STICKY HOLD - STORM DRAIN

AMBIPOM
TYPE	NORMAL
WEIGHT	20.3kg
HEIGHT	1.2m
ABILITY	PICK UP - TECHNICIAN

DRIFLOON
TYPE	GHOST - FLYING
WEIGHT	1.2kg
HEIGHT	0.4m
ABILITY	AFTERMATH - UNBURDEN

DRIFBLIM
TYPE	GHOST - FLYING
WEIGHT	15.0kg
HEIGHT	1.2m
ABILITY	AFTERMATH - UNBURDEN

BUNEARY
TYPE	NORMAL
WEIGHT	5.5kg
HEIGHT	0.4m
ABILITY	RUN AWAY - KLUTZ

LOPUNNY
TYPE	NORMAL
WEIGHT	33.3kg
HEIGHT	1.2m
ABILITY	CUTE CHARM - KLUTZ

MISMAGIUS
TYPE	GHOST
WEIGHT	4.4kg
HEIGHT	0.9m
ABILITY	LEVITATE

HONCHKROW
TYPE	DARK - FLYING
WEIGHT	27.3kg
HEIGHT	0.9m
ABILITY	INSOMNIA - SUPER LUCK

GLAMEOW
TYPE	NORMAL
WEIGHT	3.9kg
HEIGHT	0.5m
ABILITY	LIMBER - OWN TEMPO

PURUGLY
TYPE	NORMAL
WEIGHT	43.8kg
HEIGHT	1.0m
ABILITY	OWN TEMPO - THICK FAT

CHINGLING
TYPE	PSYCHIC
WEIGHT	0.6kg
HEIGHT	0.2m
ABILITY	LEVITATE

STUNKY

TYPE
POISON - DARK

WEIGHT
19.2kg

HEIGHT
0.4m

ABILITY
STENCH - AFTERMATH

SKUNTANK

TYPE
POISON - DARK

WEIGHT
38.0kg

HEIGHT
1.0m

ABILITY
STENCH - AFTERMATH

BRONZOR

TYPE
STEEL - PSYCHIC

WEIGHT
60.5kg

HEIGHT
0.5m

ABILITY
LEVEIATE - HEATPROOF

BRONZONG

TYPE
STEEL - PSYCHIC

WEIGHT
187.0kg

HEIGHT
1.3m

ABILITY
LEVITATE - HEATPROOF

BONSLY

TYPE
ROCK

WEIGHT
15.0kg

HEIGHT
0.5m

ABILITY
ROCK HEAD - STURDY

MIME JR.

TYPE
PSYCHIC

WEIGHT
13.0kg

HEIGHT
0.6m

ABILITY
SOUNDPROOF - FILTER

HAPPINY

TYPE
NORMAL

WEIGHT
24.4kg

HEIGHT
0.6m

ABILITY
NATURAL CURE - SERENE GRACE

CHATOT

TYPE
NORMAL - FLYING

WEIGHT
1.9kg

HEIGHT
0.5m

ABILITY
KEEN EYE - TANGLED FEET

SPIRITOMB

TYPE
GHOST - DARK

WEIGHT
108.0kg

HEIGHT
1.0m

ABILITY
PRESSURE

GIBLE

TYPE
DRAGON - GROUND

WEIGHT
20.5kg

HEIGHT
0.7m

ABILITY
SAND VEIL

GABITE

TYPE
DRAGON - GROUND

WEIGHT
56.0kg

HEIGHT
1.4m

ABILITY
SAND VEIL

GARCHOMP

TYPE
DRAGON - GROUND

WEIGHT
95.0kg

HEIGHT
1.9m

ABILITY
SAND VEIL

MUNCHLAX

TYPE
NORMAL

WEIGHT
105.0kg

HEIGHT
0.6m

ABILITY
PICK UP - THICK FAT

RIOLU

TYPE
FIGHTING

WEIGHT
20.2kg

HEIGHT
0.7m

ABILITY
INNER FOCUS - STEADFAST

LUCARIO

TYPE
FIGHTING - STEEL

WEIGHT
54.0kg

HEIGHT
1.2m

ABILITY
INNER FOCUS - STEADFAST

HIPPOPOTAS

TYPE
GROUND

WEIGHT
49.5kg

HEIGHT
0.8m

ABILITY
SAND STREAM

HIPPOWDON

TYPE
GROUND

WEIGHT
300.0kg

HEIGHT
2.0m

ABILITY
SAND STREAM

SKORUPI

TYPE
POISON - BUG

WEIGHT
12.0kg

HEIGHT
0.8m

ABILITY
SNIPER - BATTLE AMOUR

CONTINUED PAGE 104

ROCKY CROSSWORD

Did you enjoy Ash's latest adventure? Flick back to page 66 and relive the twists and turns of Steeling Peace of Mind! When you feel you know the action inside and out have a go at completing this story crossword.

Across

1. Dawn's next Contest is in _ _ _ _ _ _ _ _ Town.

2. Team Galactic's Commander on the island is called _ _ _ _.

3. Ash and his friends meet _ _ _ _ _, a Steel-Type specialist.

4. Both Barry and Ash are Pokémon _ _ _ _ _ _ _ _.

5. Riley's Pokémon _ _ _ _ _ _ _ protects itself with auras.

Down

1. James' most beloved Pokémon is a _ _ _ _ _ _ _ _ _.

2. A herd of Rock-Ground Type _ _ _ _ _ _ _ are driven out by Lucario.

3. Dawn, Ash and Brock travel to _ _ _ _ Island.

4. Only _ _ _ _ _ - Type Pokémon are affected by Team Galactic's operations.

5. Barry spends hours training his _ _ _ _ _ _ _ _.

PSYCHE ME OUT!

Pyschic-Type Pokémon come in all manner of colours and forms. Lucian of the Elite Four has built a vast knowledge of these fascinating Pokémon, developing an intuitive sense of the power that they can wield. Cresselia, Chimecho and Medicham may not be physically strong, but their mental force should never be underestimated!

Grab your crayons or felt-tipped pens, then bring these Psychic-Types to life! The mini poster at the bottom will show you what colours to choose.

SAVING THE WORLD
FROM RUINS!

After rushing over to Iron Island to help Barry, our Heroes find themselves confronted by a crisis of massive proportions! Team Galactic's secret activity at the ancient ruins seems to have caused all the Steel-Types on the island to act strangely. What is the evil organisation after and what is the true cause of these troubling events?

"Lucario, Stop!" shouted Ash, stepping forward to defend his new friend Riley.
Up to now, Riley's Pokémon had been the only Steel-Type to resist the strange sound wave that was corrupting the island. Now that they had got close to the source of the wave however, even Lucario couldn't resist.

Dawn screamed as Lucario turned on his former allies.
A sudden burst of power flashed from the Pokémon's spiked paw. It should have inflicted severe damage, but for some reason it glanced off the group.

"Is this… an aura?" asked Ash, looking around him.

Riley nodded. Somehow he had managed to surround them all in a protective force field strong enough to repel Lucario's attack.

"The truth is I've been training as an Aura Guardian with Lucario," explained Riley. "But there's something far more powerful than Lucario coming from those ruins. It can't protect itself against it!"
The tormented Pokémon grabbed its head, shaking with pain.

"You've gotta try and calm down," urged Brock, trying to comfort the possessed Steel-Type. Lucario repelled the Breeder with a single blow, Ash watched in horror as it summoned a lance, then began attacking small Pokémon scuttling near by. A herd of terrified Geodude were sent fleeing in all directions. When Riley tried to intervene, Lucario turned the sabre on his former master.

"Stop this, please!" shouted Ash, rushing forward to restrain the Pokémon. Brock quickly ran over to grab Lucario's free arm. While Lucario fought and kicked, Dawn helped Riley back on his feet.

"Ash, Brock!" he yelled. "Tell Pikachu to use Thunderbolt on Lucario!"

Ash gulped. "But it's in pain!"
Riley's voice went quiet. "Do it for Lucario."

Back on the Sinnoh mainland, scientists were extremely puzzled by the beam of light coming from Iron Island. A researcher in Professor Carolina's lab checked his monitor.

"A strong energy is focussing on Mount Coronet," he gasped. "It's maintaining extreme power levels."

Carolina took a moment to assess the situation. The beam was indeed making contact with the peak of Mount Coronet. After that it diffused in to shards that stretched right across the region.

"Continue to monitor it," she instructed. "We must co-ordinate with the other research facilities and collect all the data we can find."

Outside on the streets and parks of Sinnoh, local people craned their heads to watch the columns of light streaking down from the sky. Whatever energy Mars and Team Galactic had summoned, its potential was mind-blowing. Back at the source of the power surge, Barry peered up at the gleaming carvings of Palkia and Dialga. The young Trainer still couldn't quite believe that he'd got himself trapped in a pit at the bottom of these ruins. Having to share the gloomy prison with Team Rocket was even worse.

"That is not a healthy glow," said Jessie, looking up at the pulsating forms of the two legendary Pokémon.

"Perhaps not healthy for us," groaned James. Meowth pointed to the exit, far above them. "I doubt 'dey care."

The commander pressed a button and a scanner began to scroll methodically across a radar image of Mount Coronet.

"That's good," observed Cyrus. "Tell Mars to stand by."

Mars picked up the order and then signed out. Everything, it seemed, was going precisely to plan.

The welfare of Barry and Team Rocket was the last thing on Mars' mind. The Team Galactic Commander was watching her machine channel energy from the iron ruins up into the sky above her. The suffering of her captives and the thousands of Steel-Types across the island meant nothing to her.

"Headquarters?" she spoke into her headset. "G2 reporting."

Saturn picked up the connection instantly, signalling to his leader Cyrus.

"High-energy beam from Iron Island has successfully reached its target," Mars confirmed, her voice bristling with pride.

"Roger," replied Saturn. "The beam has reached Mount Coronet exactly as planned. In addition, we're detecting a powerful energy source coming directly from the mountain itself, much like the one from the island."

Cyrus swung his chair round so that he could look at the data screen in the Team Galactic command centre.

"Maintain current energy beam levels," he ordered, smiling quietly to himself.

Saturn nodded his head. "We can assume that Spear Pillar is located somewhere within this zone of energy. We are now pinpointing its precise location."

Just a few metres away from Mars, Ash was feeling the ravaging effects of Team Galactic's corrupt scheme. He and Brock were gripping onto Lucario, his frame bucking and writhing to get free.

"Use Thunderbolt while you can!" pressed Riley. "Hurry!"

Ash hesitated. Using such a powerful move on an innocent Pokémon just didn't seem right!

"I know how you feel," said Brock. "But you've got no choice."

Lucario was getting harder and harder to restrain.

Pika-chu!

The Trainer's Electric-Type tugged at his leg, its little black eyes gleaming.

"You too?" asked Ash, quickly getting the message. "OK then. Use Thunderbolt on Lucario!"

There was a blinding light and a massive bolt of power. Brock and Ash found themselves struck to the ground with the force of Pikachu's move. Lucario lay motionless for a second or two, then pulled itself upright again. The friends watched as the Pokémon sprinted straight towards the source of the sound wave.

Lucario slid down the mountainside, its eyes fixed on the iron ruins.

It leapt over the pit trapping Barry and Team Rocket, skidding to a halt in front of Mars and her precious machine. Ash and his friends followed as quickly as they could. Mars scowled when she spotted Lucario.

"These Steel-Types are so annoying!" she hissed. "Purugly, chase it away!"

Mars' Purugly launched itself at Lucario, its claws drawn. A stream of Golbat flocked around it, pounding Lucario with poisonous barbs.

"Lucario!" cried Ash, as Purugly began to slash and swipe at the Steel-Type.

Dawn covered her face as Lucario was sent sprawling across the rocks. With a final groan of anguish, the Pokémon closed its eyes.

"Lucario!" shouted Ash, his heart thumping. "We've gotta do something!"

"Not so fast," answered Riley. "Let's destroy that machine first."

Brock was beginning to understand.

"Do you think that's what's causing all the Steel-Types to be in such agony?"

"Not sure," said Riley, his eyes narrowing with concentration. "But if Lucario went in after it with such a vengeance it's got to be worth a try!"

Ash was ready and raring to go. The Trainer scooted down the gravel mountainside, desperate to take action. Riley and Brock followed behind, with Dawn bringing up the rear.

One-by-one the heroes jumped over the pit, not realising that Barry and Team Rocket were trapped below. Ash, Pikachu, Brock and Riley all made the leap, but Piplup didn't have the size for such a distance.

"Oh no!" shrieked Dawn, watching the Water-Type tumbled down the abyss.

Piplup flapped its wings, but it was too late. The Pokémon fell straight into the pit, landing with a thud in Barry's arms.

"Piplup! Are you OK?"

Dawn peered down the hole, then recoiled in surprise.

"Whaddaya know?" shouted Barry, his face beaming back up at her.

Team Rocket peered up to the light too.

"T-t-twerpette?" stuttered Jessie. "What are you all doing down there?" puzzled Dawn, signalling for Ash, Brock and Riley to go on.

The resourceful Co-ordinator quickly lowered a rope down to the group. Instead of grabbing the line with both hands however, Barry and Team Rocket started to squabble.

"It really doesn't matter who goes first!" tutted Dawn. "Somebody please just…" Too late. Before Dawn could rescue anyone a wild Steelix crashed across the rocks behind her, trapped by its own tortured mind. The rescuer was batted straight into the pit with her rescuees.

Barry's heart sank. Not only was he still trapped – now he was being squashed by a clumsy Co-ordinator!

"I'm gonna fine you for falling on me!" he pouted, thumping the ground with his fists. Dawn grimaced at the disaster.

"Uh, sorry Barry."
Meowth made a face at his pals. "I shouldda known never to trust a Twerpette!"
Team Rocket's tantrum came to a brief end when an even more troublesome problem presented itself. The incensed Steelix hovered across the opening, snapping its teeth and bashing its head against the pit walls. James clutched his Carnivine. "No matter what happens old chum, we're in this together!"
Dawn backed to the edge of pit – things were looking more desperate with every passing second!

As soon as Ash heard Dawn's scream, he turned back towards the hole.

"I'll handle this!" shouted Riley. "You guys take care of the machine!"
While Ash and Brock marched off towards the heart of the ruins, Riley watched the Steelix dart its head into the hole. Without moving a muscle, he closed his eyes and focused all the energy he could muster. Suddenly a cheer echoed out from the depths of the pit. The confused Steelix retreated at once.

Riley smiled. Amidst all the chaos on the island, he'd managed to surround Dawn and her fellow captives with a protective Aura that even a giant Steel-Type was unable to penetrate!

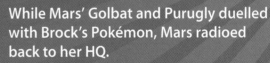

While Riley concentrated on maintaining his aura, Ash and Brock had an important job to do.

"Staravia, I choose you!" yelled Ash. Brock hurled his Poké Ball towards the sky.

"Sudowoodo, Croagunk, let's go!" The Young Trainer looked over to the spot where Lucario was still lying. Hopefully their actions would help release the Steel-Type from the sound wave's torment.

"We'll distract Team Galactic," decided Brock. "You blow that machine to bits!"

"Hang in there Lucario!" nodded Ash. "Staravia take Pikachu and get goin'!"

Pikachu leapt on to the Starling Pokémon's back, then swooped over towards Mars.

"What do they want?" barked the Commander. "Don't let them get any closer!"

"Sudowoodo!" cried Brock, right on cue. "Use Double Edge! Croagunk use Brick Break!"

While Mars' Golbat and Purugly duelled with Brock's Pokémon, Mars radioed back to her HQ.

"This is G2!" she hissed. "We have a problem!"

Ash saw his opportunity, directing Staravia towards the pulsating machine.

"Now Pikachu!" he urged. "Thunderbolt, go!"

Mars screamed in distress.

"Stop them Purugly!"

Staravia plummeted towards the evil woman using its awesome Brave Bird move. The instant they flashed past the machine, Pikachu pounded it with a super-charged bolt. The machine dissolved in black smoke.

Before Ash and Brock could celebrate, a Golbat flapped into the smoke clouds, plucking the golden key from the equipment. It dropped it neatly into Mars' hands.

"Ha!" she scoffed. "As long as we have this we'll be fine!"

As soon as the machine smashed, a calm descended on the iron ruins. The only sound came from the obelisk channelling Mars's light beam as it fell to the ground.

"Look!" whispered Barry. "The carvings of Palkia and Dialga have stopped glowing!" Dawn gasped as the Steelix gently pulled its head out of the pit. A peaceful glint came back into its eyes, as if it were waking up from a nightmare.

"It's over," marvelled Riley, retracting his protective aura.
Ash grinned when he spotted Lucario waking up too.

"That machine really was the cause," he decided. "We did it!"

Far away at Team Galactic HQ, the effect of Ash and Brock's actions was also starting to sink in.

"The energy beam has been interrupted," reported Saturn. "We currently have sixty per cent of Mount Coronet scanned, but as of this moment we have yet to locate the Spear Pillar."
Cyrus closed his eyes for a long moment.

"Instruct Mars to retreat but also make sure no one follows them," he finally replied, his voice clipped with tension.

"But do we proceed as planned?" asked Saturn.
The leader looked straight ahead.

"Obliterate them!"

Angry and frustrated, Mars followed her orders to the letter.

"Retreat at once!" she snapped, gathering a handful of valuables to take with her. Pre-trained Team Galactic operatives fetched cases of explosives from their helicopter then spread out across the iron ruins. Silently and effectively they began to tape the bombs all over the ancient shrine, priming each one to detonate in a matter of seconds.

The blades began to spin on Team Galactic's getaway vehicle. It was time for Mars to take flight.

The commander carefully placed the golden key inside the helicopter, then signalled for her soldiers to climb on board.

As soon as they heard the whir of helicopter blades, Ash, Brock and Riley ran over to check out what was going on.

"Team Galactic!" gasped Ash. "What do you want?"

Mars stopped on the chopper steps, her face filled with malice. She snatched a detonating device from a member of her crew and held it out in front of her.

"Come any closer and I'll blow up the entire island!" she warned.

Ash gasped in shock.

"Blow it up?" he asked, trying to take the words in.

Brock looked at her with disgust. "You wired everything up with bombs?"

Riley turned quietly to his Lucario. "Quickly, find them all."

"I never bluff," smirked Mars, enjoying the torment. "We don't need your world so we're simply going to destroy it, understand?"

While Mars and her crew took off from Iron Island, Ash, Brock and Riley had moments to work out their next move.

"Did Lucario locate the bombs?" asked the young Trainer.

"The explosives are all directly below the ruins," answered Riley. "Since you and Brock saved Lucario and all the other Pokémon, I would say that it's our turn now! You guys go and help your friends."

Ash and Brock waved their thanks, then ran towards the pit. They needed to figure out a way to get everyone out before any bombs went off!

By now Team Galactic's helicopter was already a safe distance from the island. Mars held the detonator in her hand and peered smugly out of the window.

"Time 'til we're safe to blow them up?" she asked.

Her pilot checked his controls. "Three minutes sir!"

Far below the chopper, Riley and Lucario were making every second count. The friends scoured the ruins for the explosives. Finally they located the devices taped onto pillars beneath the shrine.

"There are too many to even count," sighed Riley. "When Mars said that she'd destroy the island she was serious!"

While Riley and Lucario faced the challenge of everyone's lives, Ash asked Chimchar to channel a tunnel down to Dawn and the others.

"Good tinkin' Twoip!" cheered Meowth, hearing the scuffling of digging.

Dawn clapped her hands – the gloomy pit dust was playing havoc with her hair and make-up!

"Great idea guys!" she cooed, waiting to greet Chimchar's friendly face.
Instead of arriving pit-side however, the Pokémon re-appeared at Ash and Brock's feet. Its poor hands glowed with heat.

"The ground is way too hard even for Chimchar!" frowned Brock. "Digging our way out of this is not going to work."
While Ash returned the brave Pokémon to his ball, morale was getting low down below.

"Well I guess we're kaput!" announced Meowth.
James leant on his Carnivine and sobbed.

"I can't say goodbye to my mates surrounded by such drab décor!"

Carnivine listened and watched the tears flood from its master's eyes. No one noticed that the Grass-Type was getting more and more agitated, until it finally flung its vines up towards the light.

"Carni-vine!" it screeched, twisting all the way up to the top.

"Wow," said Barry. "That's Vine Whip!"
Ash sprung into action.

"All right Grotle!" he cried. "Pull up Carnivine!"
Grotle leapt through the air, clasping the vines in its powerful jaw. The Pokémon was pulled up in moments. After that it was simply a case of lifting up the prisoners one-by-one.

"Good job!" smiled Ash, as the last person was pulled up to the light.
Brock set to work treating everyone's wounds.

"It pains me woise to say this," muttered Meowth. "But tanks!"

Down in the shadows of the ruins, Riley and Lucario braced themselves.

"We've got one chance to pull this off," whispered Riley. "Let's focus."
The pair didn't have to wait for long. Two minutes' later Mars pressed the red button on her detonator device.
A unnerving low rumble thundered all across Iron Island.

"It's blowing!" cried Ash, reaching for his beloved Pikachu.

Team Rocket grabbed anyone they could find, while Dawn snapped her eyes tight shut. It was Jessie who spoke first.

"No boom?" she asked looking around her. She and all the others ought to have been blasting off by now!

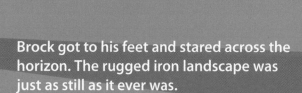

Brock got to his feet and stared across the horizon. The rugged iron landscape was just as still as it ever was.

"How is it possible?" he asked.
Way across the ocean, Mars was equally confused.

"Why aren't there any explosions?" she demanded.
There absolutely were explosions. Riley and Lucario were fighting to contain them in a giant aura sphere, resisting the dynamite with every ounce of strength that they could muster.

"Come on!" shouted Riley through gritted teeth. "Keep it up Lucario!"
Inside the aura sphere flames crashed and thundered with a terrifying force. Riley felt his arms tremble with the strain.

"Quick!" he muttered. "We have to get this away from the island now!"
Together the friends used their powers to move the sphere up and over their heads. With one last surge of effort the exploding dome was thrust into the skies. Ash and his friends cheered with relief as they watched it blow up high above their heads.

"Where's Riley and Lucario?" wondered Ash, searching the ruins below.

"Look!" cried Dawn. "Over there!" Riley and his Pokémon staggered through the smoke, their heads bent over with exhaustion. The pair were given a spontaneous heroes' welcome – even Team Rocket were knocked out by their awesome achievement!

"I can't believe that your auras were able to save the island," admired Ash, patting Riley on the back.

"Those bombs were powerful," nodded Riley. "But all's well that ends well."

Brock grinned. "I think those guys agree with you."

The group turned to see the island's Steel-Type Pokémon gathered together in

celebration. Steelix, Aggron, Magneton and Starmory all showed their appreciation for Riley and Lucario's work!

A few hours' later, Team Rocket were making their way home. To say that their stay at Iron Island had been 'interesting' was an understatement!

"Team Galactic aren't worth the gum on my shoe!" decided Jessie, looking at her team-mates.

Meowth couldn't agree more. "It's Team Rocket that rock this woild and any udda woild too!"

"Hear, hear!" agreed James. "And with Carnivine powering up with leaps and bounds, our team truly dumbfounds!"

"They may be a couple of mooshes," sniggered Jessie. "But they get an 'A' for saving the day!"

That evening, another helicopter landed on Iron Island.

"Carolina!" bellowed Ash, running up to greet the professor. "Great to see you!"

"It's the upstarts!" she grinned.

The heroes led Carolina to the ruins. After the amazing happenings of the last few days, she was fascinated to see the shrine for herself. The group walked around the site, picking up fragments from Mars' machine for Carolina to run through her laptop.

"This machine is made out of the same compound as the meteors from Veilstone City!" gasped the scientist. "Team Galactic must have made it from the materials they stole from the city park."

"It has been said that Iron Island was originally an ancient meteor," remarked Riley. "Maybe the ruins were created out of a meteor too."

"The ruins are also rumoured to reveal the location of Spear Pillar, which is necessary to summon Dialga and Palkia to this world," added Brock.

There was a silence while everyone tried to take the news in. This was monumental stuff! It was soon time for Ash and his friends to return to their travels, but Riley agreed to stay and help Carolina do some more tests on the island's structure.

A little later, Ash, Dawn and Brock were ready to take their leave. Barry and Empoleon walked the friends back down to the Iron Island ferry port.

"Man!" cried the Trainer. "Sounds like you guys got caught up in something pretty complicated!"

"I guess we did!" agreed Ash. "But now winning my next Gym Badge is all I'm gonna think about!"

Dawn giggled, then gave Barry and Empoleon a hug goodbye.

"If you happen to see Paul, tell him there's a powerful opponent waiting for him," added Barry, giving Ash a friendly wink.

"Yeah right!" grinned Ash.

Brock led the way up the gangplank. The boat back to the mainland was sailing in two minutes.

"See you!" he cried. "We'll remember to tell Paul!"

Barry laughed as he ran along the jetty. "There's a fine for you if you don't!"

With timeless experiences and memories engraved in their hearts, our Heroes board the ferry headed for Chocovine Town. For the timebeing at least, Team Galactic's ambitions have been put on indefinite hold!

LEGENDARY...
DOT·TO·DOT

Team Galactic's plot is sinister in the extreme – their actions have the potential to summon the mythical Pokémon Palkia and Dialga! The Sinnoh Legends have the power to control both space and time. Such awesome forces should only be touched by those championing good, not evil.

Bring Palkia and Dialga to life by connecting up the dots. Now colour the titans in.

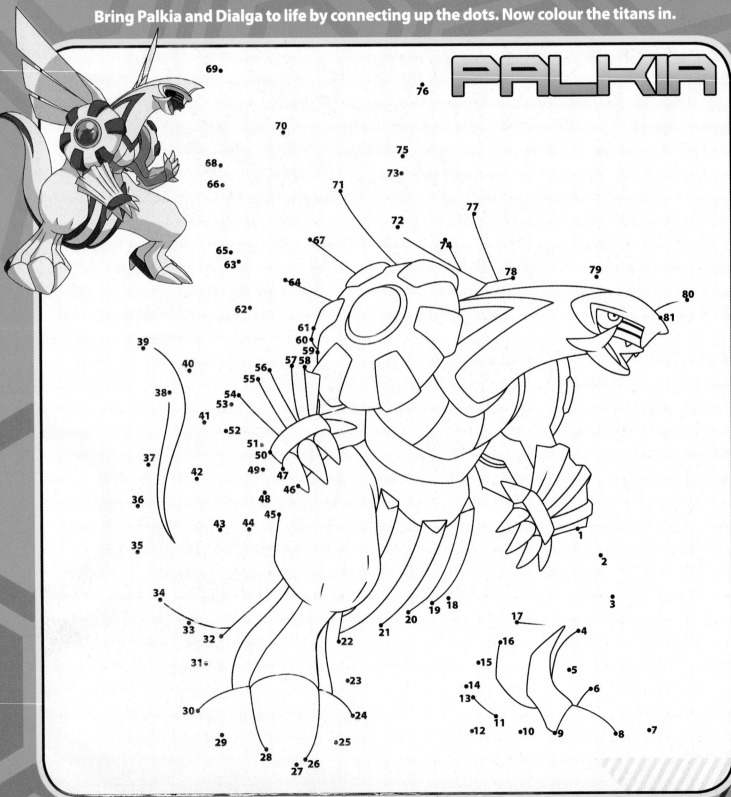

PALKIA

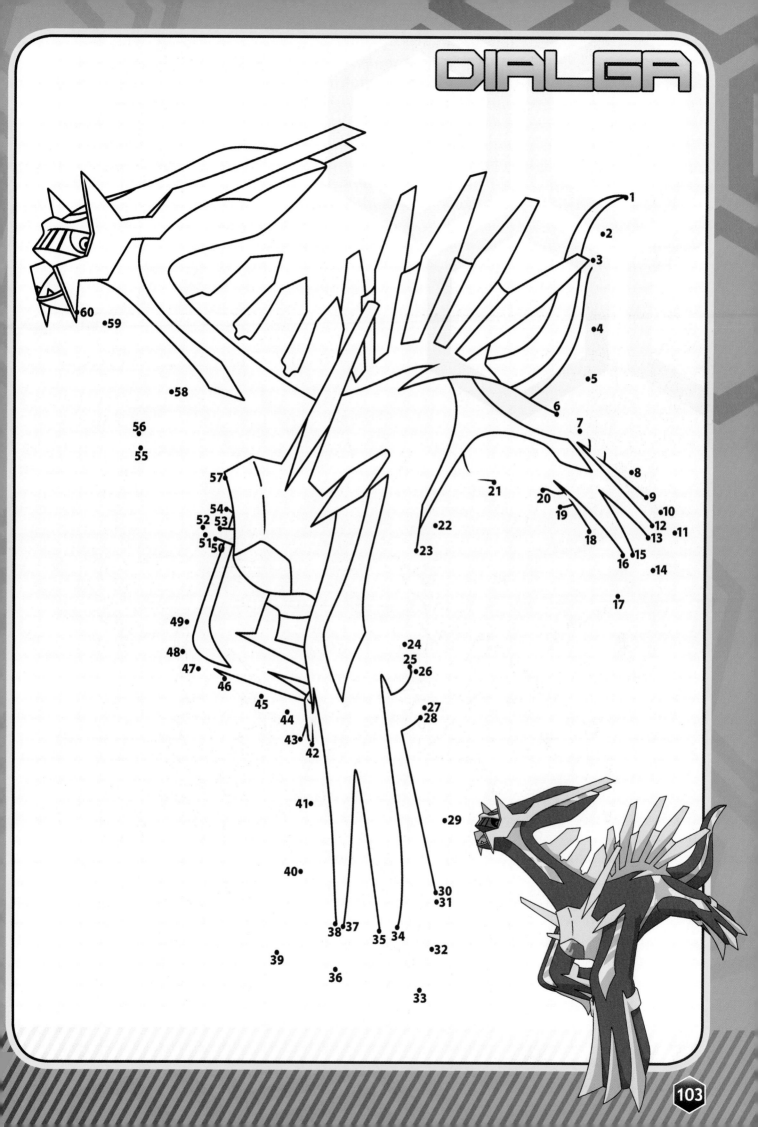

DIALGA

DRAPION

TYPE	
POISON - DARK	
WEIGHT	
61.5kg	
HEIGHT	
1.3m	
ABILITY	
SNIPER - BATTLE AMOUR	

CROAGUNK

TYPE	
POISON - FLYING	
WEIGHT	
23.0kg	
HEIGHT	
0.7m	
ABILITY	
DRY SKIN - ANTICIPATION	

TOXICROAK

TYPE	
POISON - FIGHTING	
WEIGHT	
44.4kg	
HEIGHT	
1.3m	
ABILITY	
DRY SKIN - ANTICIPATION	

CARNIVINE

TYPE	
GRASS	
WEIGHT	
27.0kg	
HEIGHT	
1.4m	
ABILITY	
LEVITATE	

FINNEON

TYPE	
WATER	
WEIGHT	
7.0kg	
HEIGHT	
0.4m	
ABILITY	
SWIFT SWIM - STORM DRAIN	

LUMINEON

TYPE	
WATER	
WEIGHT	
24.0kg	
HEIGHT	
1.2m	
ABILITY	
SWIFT SWIM - STORM DRAIN	

MANTYKE

TYPE	
WATER - FLYING	
WEIGHT	
65.0kg	
HEIGHT	
1.0m	
ABILITY	
WATER ABSORB - SWIFT SWIM	

SNOVER

TYPE	
GRASS - ICE	
WEIGHT	
50.5kg	
HEIGHT	
1.0m	
ABILITY	
SNOW - WARNING	

ABOMASNOW

TYPE	
GRASS - ICE	
WEIGHT	
135.5kg	
HEIGHT	
2.2m	
ABILITY	
SNOW - WARNING	

WEAVILE

TYPE	
DARK - ICE	
WEIGHT	
34.0kg	
HEIGHT	
1.1m	
ABILITY	
PRESSURE	

MAGNEZONE

TYPE	
ELECTRIC - STEEL	
WEIGHT	
180.0kg	
HEIGHT	
1.2m	
ABILITY	
STURDY - MAGNET PULL	

LICKILICKY

TYPE	
NORMAL	
WEIGHT	
140.0kg	
HEIGHT	
1.7m	
ABILITY	
OBLIVIOUS - OWN TEMPO	

RHYPERIOR

TYPE	
GROUND - ROCK	
WEIGHT	
282.8kg	
HEIGHT	
2.4m	
ABILITY	
LIGHTNING ROD - SOLID ROCK	

TANGROWTH

TYPE	
GRASS	
WEIGHT	
128.6kg	
HEIGHT	
2.0m	
ABILITY	
CHLOROPHYLL - LEAF GUARD	

ELECTIVIRE

TYPE	
ELECTRIC	
WEIGHT	
138.6kg	
HEIGHT	
1.8m	
ABILITY	
MOTOR DRIVE	

MAGMORTAR

TYPE	
FIRE	
WEIGHT	
68.0kg	
HEIGHT	
1.6m	
ABILITY	
FLAME BODY	

TOGEKISS

TYPE	
NORMAL - FLYING	
WEIGHT	
38.0kg	
HEIGHT	
1.5m	
ABILITY	
SERENE GRACE - HUSTLE	

YANMEGA

TYPE	
BUG - FLYING	
WEIGHT	
51.5kg	
HEIGHT	
1.9m	
ABILITY	
TINTED LENS - SPEED BOOST	

TYPE
GRASS

WEIGHT
25.5kg

HEIGHT
1.0m

ABILITY
LEAF GUARD

TYPE
ICE

WEIGHT
25.9kg

HEIGHT
0.8m

ABILITY
SNOW CLOAK

TYPE
GROUND - FLYING

WEIGHT
42.5kg

HEIGHT
2.0m

ABILITY
SAND VEIL - HYPER CUTTER

MAMOSWINE

TYPE
ICE - GROUND

WEIGHT
291.0kg

HEIGHT
2.5m

ABILITY
OBLIVIOUS - SNOW CLOAK

PORYGON - 2

TYPE
NORMAL

WEIGHT
34.0kg

HEIGHT
0.9m

ABILITY
ADAPTABILITY - DOWNLOAD

GALLADE

TYPE
PSYCHIC - FIGHTING

WEIGHT
52.0kg

HEIGHT
1.6m

ABILITY
STEADFAST

PROBOPASS

TYPE
ROCK - STEEL

WEIGHT
340.0kg

HEIGHT
1.4m

ABILITY
STURDY - MAGNET PULL

DUSKNOIR

TYPE
GHOST

WEIGHT
106.6kg

HEIGHT
2.2m

ABILITY
PRESSURE

FROSLASS

TYPE
ICE - GHOST

WEIGHT
26.6kg

HEIGHT
1.3m

ABILITY
SNOW CLOAK

ROTOM

TYPE
ELECTRIC - GHOST

WEIGHT
0.3kg

HEIGHT
0.3m

ABILITY
LEVITATE

UXIE

TYPE
PSYCHIC

WEIGHT
0.3kg

HEIGHT
0.3m

ABILITY
LEVITATE

MESPRIT

TYPE
PSYCHIC

WEIGHT
0.3kg

HEIGHT
0.3m

ABILITY
LEVITATE

AZELF

TYPE
PSYCHIC

WEIGHT
0.3kg

HEIGHT
0.3m

ABILITY
LEVITATE

DIALGA

TYPE
STEEL - DRAGON

WEIGHT
683.0kg

HEIGHT
5.4m

ABILITY
PRESSURE

PALKIA

TYPE
WATER - DRAGON

WEIGHT
336.0kg

HEIGHT
4.2m

ABILITY
PRESSURE

HEATRAN

TYPE
FIRE - STEEL

WEIGHT
430.0kg

HEIGHT
1.7m

ABILITY
FLASH FIRE

REGIGIGAS

TYPE
NORMAL

WEIGHT
420.0kg

HEIGHT
3.7m

ABILITY
SLOW START

GIRATINA

ORIGIN FORME

TYPE
GHOST - DRAGON

WEIGHT
650.0kg

HEIGHT
6.9m

ABILITY
LEVITATE

TYPE
GHOST - DRAGON
WEIGHT
750.0kg
HEIGHT
4.5m
ABILITY
PRESSURE

TYPE
PSYCHIC
WEIGHT
85.6kg
HEIGHT
1.5m
ABILITY
LEVITATE

TYPE
WATER
WEIGHT
3.1kg
HEIGHT
0.4m
ABILITY
HYDRATION

MANAPHY

TYPE
WATER
WEIGHT
0.3kg
HEIGHT
1.4m
ABILITY
HYDRATION

DARKRAI

TYPE
DARK
WEIGHT
50.5kg
HEIGHT
1.5m
ABILITY
BAD DREAMS

SHAYMIN — LAND FORME

TYPE
GRASS
WEIGHT
2.1kg
HEIGHT
0.2m
ABILITY
NATURAL CURE

SHAYMIN — SKY FORME

TYPE
GRASS - FLYING
WEIGHT
5.2kg
HEIGHT
0.4m
ABILITY
SERENE GRACE

ARCEUS

TYPE
NORMAL
WEIGHT
320.0kg
HEIGHT
3.2m
ABILITY
MULTI-TYPE

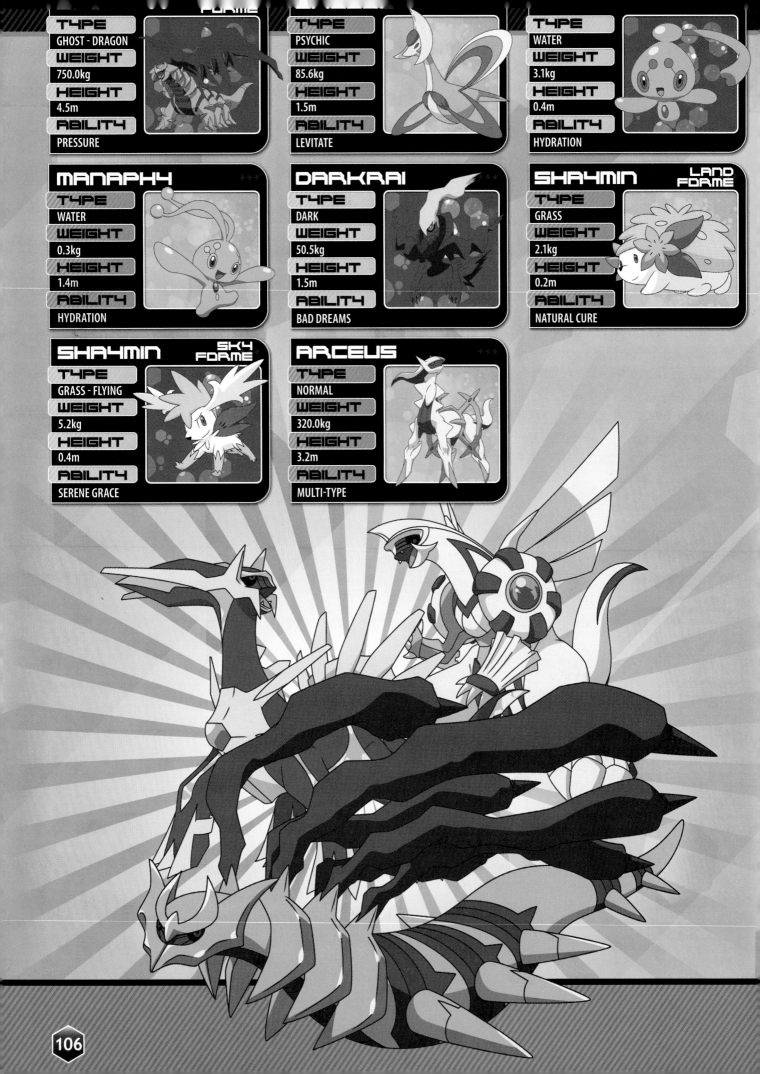

POKÉDEX CRASH!

Ash's Pokédex has crashed just when he needs it most! Help the Trainer get round the glitch by matching the Pokémon below with their correct profile information.

A

ONCE IT APPEARS, ITS FURY WON'T ABATE UNTIL IT HAS CAUSED TOTAL DESTRUCTION

TOGEPI

GYARADOS

B

IT IS NOTORIOUSLY FICKLE, SWITCHING FROM PURRS TO SNARLS IN A MATTER OF SECONDS.

A = ??????????????
B = ??????????????
C = ??????????????
D = ??????????????
E = ??????????????

C

IT IS GENEROUS AND KIND-HEARTED. ITS SHELL IS BELIEVED TO BE STUFFED WITH HAPPINESS.

PIPLUP

E

THE ELECTRIC POUCHES ON ITS CHEEKS ARE USED FOR STORING STATIC CHARGE.

PICHU

D

IT HAS A THICK DOWN OF FEATHERS TO PROTECT IT FROM THE COLD.

GLAMEOW

ANSWERS

ULTIMATE SINNOH POKÉDEX

THE MISSING POKÉDEX PROFILE BELONGS TO PIKACHU:

025 – PIKACHU
TYPE: Electric **ABILITY:** Static
HEIGHT: 0.4m **WEIGHT:** 6.0kg

PAGE 12: POKÉ PRACTICE!

1-**A** 2-**B** 3-**C** 4-**A** 5-**B**
6-**C** 7-**C** 8-**A** 9-**A** 10-**C**

PAGE 13: SMALL AND PERFECTLY FORMED!

1. AZURILL **2.** DRIFLOON
3. PICHU **4.** EEVEE

PAGE 14: TYPE TRIALS

1-**D** 2-**E** 3-**A** 4-**F** 5-**B** 6-**C**

PAGE 15: SINNOH WORDSEARCH

T	M	I	R	O	N	I	S	L	A	N	D	D	U
W	E	X	J	O	X	I	T	M	V	X	K	E	T
I	S	N	O	W	P	O	I	N	T	C	I	T	Y
N	P	Z	O	W	E	D	Y	F	G	L	V	E	S
L	E	D	C	R	S	D	I	H	J	A	P	R	X
E	A	M	C	Q	O	J	V	O	L	K	R	N	K
A	R	G	B	J	K	C	M	K	P	E	K	A	R
F	P	A	W	B	F	K	T	I	H	V	P	C	A
T	I	R	H	T	Y	N	K	N	T	A	M	I	P
O	L	D	C	H	A	T	E	A	U	L	L	T	L
W	L	Q	R	J	B	P	G	K	H	O	A	Y	A
N	A	G	J	K	Q	H	M	A	D	R	M	M	P
T	R	O	P	H	Y	G	A	R	D	E	N	O	X

PAGE 30: MATCH THE MOVES

ASH
CHIMCHAR – Flamethrower
BUIZEL – Water Gun
GLISCOR – Steel Wing

BYRON
BRONZOR – Raindance
STEELIX – Iron Tail
BASTIODON – Metal Burst

PAGES 36 - 39: GRAND TRAINER CHALLENGE!

PART ONE – POKÉMON KNOWLEDGE
1. Magmar, **2.** Gligar, **3.** Eevee
4. Manaphy (because it is not in the same evolution chain)
5. Snorunt, **6.** Clefairy, **7.** Psychic, **8.** Chansey

PART TWO – OBSERVATION
1. Mamoswine, **2.** Geodude, **3.** Sudowoodo
4. Wurmple, **5.** HootHoot, **6.** Combee
7. Psyduck, **8.** Turtwig

PART THREE – COMBAT SKILLS
1. Aura shields, **2.** Poison, **3.** True,
4. Bubblebeam, **5.** It works in a pack,
6. Staraptor, **7.** Machoke, **8.** Thunderbolt

PART FOUR – BATTLE GYMS
1. COAL Badge, **2. ICICLE** Badge, **3. RELIC** Badge
4. BEACON Badge, **5. COBBLE** Badge
6. FOREST Badge, **7. MINE** Badge, **8. FEN** Badge

PAGE 54: SPARKY SPOTS

PAGE 55: MURKY MAZE

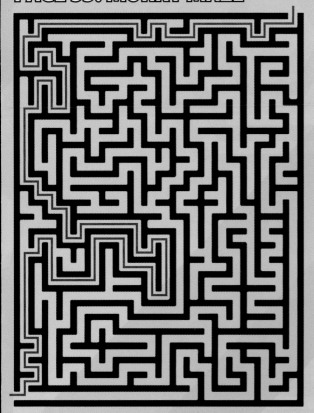

PAGE 56: MISSING LINKS

1. LICKITUNG **2.** GASTLY **3.** TENTACRUEL
4. PIKACHU **5.** TANGELA **6.** TORTERRA

PAGE 57: EVOLUTION SOLUTIONS

RAMPARDOS HAS…

1. Dark blue rings around its arms.
2. Two large side horns on its head.
3. Sharp spines protruding from each knee.
4. Dark red eyes.
5. A blue neck band with spines at each side.
6. Extra height – Rampardos is taller than Cranidos.
7. Four short head spines.
8. An extended tale with a dark blue flash band.
9. A darker charcoal coloured body.
10. Two sharp fangs.

CRANIDOS AND RAMPARDOS HAVE…

1. A powerful hard skull **2.** Two-legged posture

PAGE 59: SHY SHADOWS

1. BUNEARY **2.** TOGEKISS **3.** FROSLASS
4. ABRA **5.** PILOSWINE **6.** UMBREON

PAGES 64 - 65: THE POKÉMON A-Z

There is no Pokémon starting with the letter **X**.
(Xatu starts with the letter X but it is a Johto Pokémon)

PAGE 86 : ROCKY CROSSWORD

		G		I								
		E		R								
C	H	O	C	O	V	I	N	E				
A		D		N			M	A	R	S		
R		U					P					
N		D				R	O	I	L	E	Y	
I		E					E					
V				S			O					
I			T	R	A	I	N	E	R	S		
N				E								
E				E								
			L	U	C	A	R	I	O			

PAGE 107: POKÉDEX CRASH!

1. C **2.** A **3.** E **4.** B **5.** D